"Marley."

Keti hugs the dog.

Oh, thank God! This is her room, in her house, and she is *alive*.

It's Christmas Eve, and she's been given another chance.

Suddenly there is no time. But not in the sense that there's been no time in the past—no time for anything but work.

There isn't time enough to do all the things she wants to do before Christmas Day dawns…. Time to find gifts, to see all the people she needs to see. Time to change the future—since she can't change the past.

Dear Reader,

What makes Christmas? In each family, in each person's life, traditions are different. I love to go to Mass on Christmas Eve. I must watch *Rudolph, the Red-Nosed Reindeer* at least once. And I'm filled with yule spirit by reading Charles Dickens's *A Christmas Carol*.

It was a challenge and a pleasure to write a Harlequin Everlasting Love novel embroidering plot, theme and words from Dickens's work. From the beginning, I wanted my contemporary Scrooge character to be female, a woman who had acquired great power in business. In the original tale, Scrooge bypassed romance; by the end, it was known that he always kept Christmas well, yet he missed so much in life along the way—including marriage and children. I wanted Keti Whitechapel, my Scrooge, to have her chance at love, and I wanted her life to build and grow as her generosity reawakened.

I hope you enjoy this Christmas story, and I wish you and yours the happiest of holidays. Many thanks to Mr. Dickens for writing his timeless book.

Sincerely,
Margot Early

A SPIRIT OF CHRISTMAS

MARGOT EARLY

HARLEQUIN®

TORONTO • NEW YORK • LONDON
AMSTERDAM • PARIS • SYDNEY • HAMBURG
STOCKHOLM • ATHENS • TOKYO • MILAN • MADRID
PRAGUE • WARSAW • BUDAPEST • AUCKLAND

ISBN-13: 978-0-373-65424-6
ISBN-10:   0-373-65424-3

A SPIRIT OF CHRISTMAS

www.eHarlequin.com

Printed in U.S.A.

ABOUT THE AUTHOR

Margot Early lives high in Colorado's San Juan Mountains with two German shepherds and other pets. She is happiest when close to nature, jogging and bike riding in the mountains. Her interests include belly dance, midwifery and spinning. A lover of myth and saga, she feels profoundly grateful for the opportunity to write stories.

For Mary Beth

Chapter 1

Keti Whitechapel never intended to end up in Bounty, Nevada. In fact, when she was a child, she wanted nothing more than to get out of Bounty at the earliest opportunity. And she did.

At fifty-five, she's been just about everywhere but the moon, and now she's back in town. She owns the Bounty Mountain Resort, whose world-class skiing rivals Switzerland's St. Moritz, and the Empress Mine, whose rich deposits of gold give employment to three hundred miners. She owns an Idaho silver mine and Bounty's largest casino. There are LLCs, too, and almost two percent of the NASDAQ. She used to own a couple of brothels, as well.

So she's back in Bounty, no longer the poor buck-toothed daughter of a hard-drinking, hard-playing hard-rock miner, but the woman who owns it all. The woman who's known locally as the Queen.

And it's Christmas Eve, with a fog so dense it's hard to see the porch from the sidewalk. A Mexican laborer is shoveling the long walk up to Keti's house. Her motion lights pick out his shape and the curl of steam from his breath, and when he sees her step out of the Hummer at the curb he shifts onto the snowy lawn to allow her to pass. Somewhere north of town, out on the highway, sirens sound.

Keti swings her black leather tote over her shoulder, shuts her car door and locks it automatically. She prefers to drive herself. She prefers to be alone, period. If you live alone, it's better to protect yourself. Keti owns several handguns and practices with them regularly. As far as she's concerned, she needs no one.

The wrought-iron gate by the sidewalk stands open, and she hurries through.

"Merry Christmas," says the worker, leaning on his shovel.

What reason do you have to be merry? she wonders as she nods. *You're poor.* But at least he speaks English. She instructs him, "Make sure there's no ice, and if that mangy animal across the street has been over here again, I don't want to step in anything." The mutt is, like many in Bounty, owned by people Keti thinks of as the Great Unwashed. Trust-fund kids with uncombed hair who look like runaways from a Grateful Dead show and talk about healing and auras and live on alfalfa sprouts and are only outnumbered by their dogs, which Keti hasn't yet managed to ban from Bounty. The canine across the street is black and white and overweight and he thinks her lawn is his toilet. But all of Bounty's dogs seem to fear Keti: when they see her approaching, they tug their owners into doorways. Away from her, which is how she likes it.

The man with the shovel asks Keti, in Spanish, if she speaks Spanish. She does, quite well—she grew up a miner's daughter in Bounty, after all. But now she simply shrugs in exasperation. Once she was friendly with her workers, but eventually she saw how careful she would have to be. Everyone wants money—her money. They want to know her and befriend her so that she will subsidize them or, worse, so that they can blackmail or sue her. Once, she thought people who believed such things were paranoid or suffered from delusions of grandeur. But life has taught her. Oh, how she's learned.

She stalks past the man, glad at least that her property manager, a fluffy little thing, Tiffany, who is Martin Collins's niece, has made sure someone keeps the walk clear.

Martin, Martin, Martin.

Keti refuses to think about Martin. And yet she knows she will.

But later.

A tall cardboard box leans against the jamb of the front door, almost crushing the wreath that someone has hung for Keti, obscuring the knocker that used to hang on the home of Bounty's first miner baron—the man who owned the Empress Mine when Keti's father worked there. Keti is annoyed by the wreath. The porch light catches the brass knocker, which was actually brought from England by the miner baron. It is shaped like an eagle-bird-lion creature, a griffin, she supposes. But at the moment it doesn't look like a griffin. Instead, it resembles Aunt Marlene's face.

Keti blinks, and it's a griffin once again.

She turns her attention to the huge box propped up beside her. The return address is Las Vegas and Keti knows what's inside. A momentary disappointment, something she doesn't want to analyze, gives way to satisfaction. Well, at least it's finally here.

Her aunt's mirror.

Keti doesn't want to think about the fact that Marlene is dead, because Marlene was the one person Keti has loved who never turned her back on Keti; never chose others over Keti. And now she's gone.

Marlene actually wasn't her aunt but her great-aunt, which Keti thinks explains why the two of them got along so well. They had an understanding about certain things. When Keti first met her, Marlene was the madam of a brothel just outside Las Vegas. Keti herself would soon begin working underground in the Empress Mine, and prove herself in an environment profoundly hostile to women.

But then Marlene took her out of the mine and showed her how to make far more money at much less cost to herself. It was Marlene who taught her to be a successful businesswoman.

You loved me, Keti thinks again. *You really loved me, Marlene, and you looked after me.*

Yes, the mirror is part of her inheritance, and it isn't a surprise. It's not exactly a present, but it arrived on Christmas Eve, so it feels a bit like a post-humous Christmas gift from Marlene.

Her breath fogs before her as she inserts her key in the lock. Inside, she disarms the alarm system. Then she steps back to retrieve the mirror, but it's heavy. Still, she wants it upstairs, and she wants it upstairs now. The miner baron's house, Bonanza Victorian–style, has been completely renovated, but Keti had certainly never thought to install an elevator. How is she going to carry that mirror up the narrow staircase by herself?

"You want help?"

The Mexican. If he can speak English, why did he ask her if she could speak Spanish?

"Sí." It isn't what she'd intended to say. She doesn't let strangers into her house, and she doesn't speak Spanish with the migrant laborers. Only occasionally, with their wives.

As he picks up the box, he remarks that it weighs a lot, and she asks him, in Spanish, where he is from.

"Chihuahua." And more detail. His village. His brother and sister-in-law will join him in Nevada that summer. His wife works in one of Bounty's hotels. They are expecting their third child. His wife has only a little English. He is going to classes. And he switches back to English, to practice.

Keti does not ask about his wife. She has seen the woman, whose baby has already dropped; who is undoubtedly due any day. It is not her concern. Probably, the woman is one of Martin's patients, and Keti does *not* intend to think about Martin. She has trained herself not to think about him, and she's gotten fairly good at it.

Reluctantly, she turns on a couple of lights so that the man can see to go upstairs. Darkness is economical, and Keti believes it's a good thing to be used to. Especially for anyone in mining, even a mine owner.

She hears a low animal whine from somewhere toward the back of the house.

The Mexican tells her, "It's a dog. He has…" He gestures to his face. "What do you say?"

She does not recognize the next word he uses.

He says, "Points. Animal."

She shrugs, uncomprehending.

He touches his chest. "Thin. Bones."

The dog, she presumes, and anyway, it has nothing to do with her. "I'll call the marshal," she says. Bounty's answer to animal control.

A sad look crosses the man's face.

He carries the heavy carton upstairs to the master bedroom, which faces the street, keeping a respectful distance from his employer. There is no reason for Keti to be distrustful, except that she knows inviting *any* stranger into her home is foolish. There are too many bad people in the world, and *no one* can tell the good from the bad. What is the use of having lived the kind of life she has, if she hasn't learned that?

He asks if she wants the mirror taken out of the box, but she shakes her head. She wants to do that herself. Before she follows him downstairs, Keti turns off her bedroom light, again, and then the hall light. At the front door, she tells him, "I want to give you some money."

"No." He waves away the suggestion. "No. Thank you."

"You can send it to your family."

"No. No."

She presses a bill into his hand, change from a latte she bought just after she'd arrived at the airport.

He says, "Thank you," and takes the dollar, looking down and then nodding again. "Merry Christmas."

He steps out the door with only the merest backward glance, but that glance is like a mirror in which Keti sees herself. Again.

Suddenly she is that bucktoothed miner's daughter once more. And as she starts to close the door, she sees Marlene's face. She slams it shut and turns out the last light in the foyer.

But there's that damn animal, whining again and scratching.

She sets her alarms in total darkness, walks into the kitchen, with its restaurant-quality stove, refrigerator, espresso-maker and everything she might ever want. Something is on the table, a poinsettia, she thinks, no doubt also left by that ridiculous Tiffany, who hasn't the money to spare on such nonsense. Keti reminds herself to take off her boots, and is annoyed when she remembers that she didn't ask the Mexican to remove his footwear before carrying the mirror upstairs. Now she regrets giving him any money. Picking up her cordless phone, she dials 13, her speed-dialing code for the town marshal. Dispatch, not emergency.

"Bounty marshal's office."

"It's Keti Whitechapel. There's a stray over here, whining and scratching."

"I'm sorry, but I really don't have anyone to send. There's a multiple-car accident over by Society Turn."

"All right."

"Merry Christmas."

"Yes. Good night."

She glances at the pointsettia and makes out a card beside it, colored by one of Tiffany's fatherless brood. Though Tiffany did actually marry the last one, the father of the child with all the problems. The card reads, in Tiffany's hand, "Dine with us tomorrow."

Pretentious. The last time they'd talked, Keti had asked Tiffany, *Why did you get married?* After all, the man doesn't make enough money for them to live on, and yet marrying him has reduced Tiffany's government benefits.

Martin's silly niece, her silly goddaughter, had said, *Because I fell in love.*

Because you fell in love! Keti snorts at the recollection.

She goes through to the back of the house. The damn animal is banging on her screen. For all she knows, it might even be rabid.

Deciding not to open the door after all, she heads upstairs. If she ignores it, maybe it will go away. There is a Leatherman tool in her vanity drawer, and she uses the sharpest, largest knife on it to cut open the box enclosing the mirror. Then she unpacks the paper that surrounds it, making a mess on her floor.

The ornate frame is cherry, carved with a pattern of roses—wild-looking roses. It stands over six feet tall, and the oval of the mirror itself tilts on its frame. She positions it from the back and so can't miss the envelope that is taped there.

She recognizes the paper, because Marlene always wrote on the same pale peach linen paper and used dark rose linen envelopes. Her name, Ketura—an old family name—is written on it in Marlene's hand.

A letter?

Keti wants to keep the envelope attached to the mirror, and she wonders if it is actually sealed and if she can open it without removing it. She slides her finger behind and finds it is taped in place with a loop of duct tape.

Oh, well.

She removes it, and there is Marlene's wax seal on the back, the last seal of hers that Keti will ever open.

She has letter openers and she has the Leatherman, but she uses neither. Just her fingers, short-nailed and plain, because that is how she prefers them. No rings, either.

Photos.

Snapshots taken with a cheap camera, and now the color is faded, but Keti recognizes the people. Two children on swings, in the park in Bounty—a girl, probably five years old, with thick, tangled golden hair, and a dark-haired boy in a striped T-shirt and cheap blue jeans.

Martin.

Of course.

Martin, the boy, who became Martin, the only man she has ever loved. Martin, whom she will not see this Christmas because she's done with him, done with his fluffy niece and done with the entire sentimental good-deed-doing Collins family.

She returns all the photos to the envelope and sets the envelope on her dresser, then walks around the mirror to stand before it.

She's in good shape, she supposes, for fifty-five. She was always a solid woman. Five foot five, with enough bust and rather too much rear end. Her teeth are white and straight, though the road to having them straightened was complicated. She has never fixed her one chipped tooth, however, because she rather likes it. For years she'd smiled with a closed mouth. Then, for a brief while, she smiled fully.

She sees no reason to smile now.

She gets highlights—sometimes low lights—and

she takes care of herself, works out. And still she looks old.

Would that animal go away?

She hears something banging about in her backyard.

I'll throw water on it.

She pauses on the stairs to turn down the in-floor heating, then walks through the shadowy kitchen and grabs one of her copper pots, which she fills with cold water.

She goes to the back door, punches in the code to deactivate the alarm, and opens the door. The yard is so dark that even Keti, who knows every square inch of it, is reluctant to grope with her hands. She won't touch the creature, whatever it is. She will throw water on it and it will leave.

But the animal is bumping against the screen, *ruining* the screen, and it's whimpering. It appears to be stuck to the mesh.

With porcupine quills.

Good grief. That's what the Mexican meant when he referred to "points."

She has to get it unstuck from the door. It smells as if it's had an encounter with a skunk at some point, too, and Keti's not one hundred percent sure that it's a domestic animal at all. The mutt has huge ears, one of which bends forward at the tip, and it looks a bit like a coyote—though with pale blue eyes—and a bit like one of those cow dogs she's always seeing in the backs of pickup trucks. It has no tail, and it's gray with black spots and some kind of cinnamon color on its nose and ears. No collar, of course.

She sets down the pot and tries to open her door, and the canine backs up, squealing, then wrenches itself free.

Keti wastes no time. She lifts the pot of water and hurls it at the dog.

It doesn't yelp but backs away, then shakes itself, and lies down on the back porch, looking at her, its face full of quills.

Good God.

It is skeletally thin. Keti wonders if pound dogs die by lethal injection or if they're gassed.

"It's obvious," she says, "why you got skunked and porcupined. You don't understand when you're not wanted."

It's not that she hates dogs. She hates *particular* dogs. And she particularly hates the *owners* of *particular* dogs, like that moron down the road who lets his border collie play tag with cars. That dog of his is going to cause an accident one day soon.

She steps onto the porch, deciding that it really is a dog and that it's not rabid. Instinctively, she grabs a quill and pulls.

It comes out. The dog stands up.

Good. Maybe if she tries to pull out the remaining quills, it will leave.

She knows how to do this. She's done it before—just not for decades.

She stands over the dog, pressing her knees against its neck, and it squirms. She grabs the quills and she pulls. She removes about eighteen this way, her hands growing cold as the dog tries to pull her off the porch. But he's no match for her. She is strong and healthy and this dog has been starved. The quills on its chin present the greatest challenge. Then, all that's left is its nose.

As it cries, wriggling hysterically, she says calmly, "Just cool it."

There are no quills in its throat, so maybe it's not a seasoned, obsessed, maniacal hunter of porcupines.

"You're not getting loose until I get every one of these."

The dog reeks.

"Dammit. Ow."

Fifteen minutes later the animal is inside the master bathroom, standing in the tiled shower beside her. There is a bench, and Keti has a bottle of Bloody Mary mix at hand, which she dumps on the dog beneath the warm spray.

The dog doesn't fight the shower or try to escape, but instead puts his feet on her knees.

Her eyes begin to water.

She calls him Marley, for the last person who loved her, then says to him, "I bet you've never slept on a memory-foam mattress."

She sees, in her mind, the photograph she did not want to see, and pictures an older version of the boy on the swing beside hers. A much more recent, more present-time Martin. She blinks away the image and pets the dog.

Chapter 2

Keti awakens to the tolling of a bell. She hasn't been asleep long. She can't have been, for when she turns on her smallest Arts and Crafts stained-glass lamp, with its energy-saving bulb, the glass-domed clock on her dresser reads midnight, and the sound of the bell is from the church down the street. It must be. Announcing Christmas.

The first Christmas, for many years, that she won't see Martin Collins.

She has chosen not to.

The dog lifts his head and looks at her. One huge ear stands straight up and the other falls over.

"Merry Christmas, Marley," she says, gazing at the mirror.

Impulsively, she climbs out of bed to retrieve the envelope of photographs. Marley, who has quickly adjusted to memory foam, remains where he lies, watching her intently.

Why did you give me these pictures, Marlene? Keti wonders as she climbs back into bed. *I don't want to look back. Not to those times. Not to any of them.*

She holds the small stack of photos, puts the one of Martin and her on the swings behind the others, and sees what is next.

Beside her, Marley whimpers, then gives a sharp bark, but Keti sees only the photo before her.

Martin, Martin again, sharing a milk shake with Keti, one glass, two straws, on the brick patio of what used to be the Bounty General Store and is now the extremely upscale Bounty Mercantile. In this old photo Keti's teeth stick out so far it is no wonder she finally chipped one. *I was a mess,* she thinks, shuddering at the contrast between herself, so obviously impoverished, and Martin, handsome and well cared for.

She looks at another snapshot. Keti and Martin skating on the rink at Town Park, playing hockey with homemade sticks. Back when they were more like brother and sister than anything else.

She puts away the photos again and glances at the mirror as she sets them on the nightstand. Then she looks back, a double take. There is someone there, standing before the mirror, looking into it, someone not completely solid, but nearly so. A woman with white hair, pinned in elaborate braids atop her head. She wears a red Chanel suit and Italian pumps, and she is old, very old.

Marlene?

Keti touches her own skin, and then rests her hand on the warm dog, Marley. This can't be a dream... But it is dreamlike.

Marlene turns.

"What do you want with me?" Keti is only half-surprised the words come from her. Aunt Marlene is dead—this can't be her.

"Much!"

Marlene's voice. This thing, this being, *wants* something.

Marley whimpers and barks again. Keti keeps a hand on him. "Who are you?" she asks.

"In life, I was Marlene Whitechapel, your father's aunt." She glances at the end of Keti's bed.

Keti says, "You can sit there. If you *can* sit."

The woman in red sits on the edge of the bed. She is shrunken by the passage of decades, withered and unwanted. She can't be Marlene, though she does look like her. Her hands are cuffed together at the wrists. Keti thinks of the Nevada brothels. Marlene's Nevada brothels. And those she herself owned for a time, giving Martin a gold-plated invitation to act holier-than-thou.

Marley bares his teeth.

"It's okay," Keti tells him, though she isn't sure she means it.

"Do you believe in me?" asks the ghost.

"I think this is a dream. Why else would you have come to me?"

"It is required of every person," her visitor answers, "that the spirit within him should walk among his fellow creatures and travel far and wide. If one doesn't do this in life, one is condemned to do so after death. I am doomed to wander through the world and witness what I can't share, but might have shared on earth and turned to happiness!"

"Why are you wearing handcuffs?"

"I wear the chains I forged in life," Marlene's shadow replies. "Do you know the fetters you bear, Keti?"

Fetters? "What do you mean? This is not comforting."

"I have no comfort to give, Keti. No regret can make amends for missing the opportunity that life offers."

"But you lived a full life, Marlene." Keti wants to console the ghost of the older woman she loved. "You were a successful businesswoman at a time when women in business were resented even more than they are now. You achieved your goals."

"Goals! Business! Mankind should have been my business, Keti. Charity, mercy, forbearance and benevolence. But instead I made money my business. Don't you see?"

Keti remembers the Mexican worker who shoveled her walk and the way he'd looked at her after she gave him that single dollar bill. As if *he* was sorry for *her.*

"Listen to me, Keti. My time with you is nearly gone."

"I'm listening." And quaking. Marley shivers at her side, ears back, head slunk low.

"I am here tonight to warn you," says the ghost, "that you have yet a chance to escape my fate. I am giving you this chance, and it is only my love for you in life that allows me this opportunity to escape the torment I will otherwise endure."

This is a dream. I'll wake up, Keti thinks. The word *torment* makes her think of Martin. Martin doesn't love her, won't love her; and that is her torment.

"You will be visited by three spirits," the ghost informs her.

"I'd rather not be."

"Do you want to share my fate, Keti, condemned to wander the earth because you didn't learn to love and to care in life?"

"I know how to love and care!" She touches

Marley, reminding herself that she rescued him just that night.

And she has rescued *people* before. Oh, Martin might not see it that way. Or maybe he thinks she should spend *all* her time rescuing people.

He definitely thinks she should be someone other than the woman she is.

He has always wanted her to be different and he has never stopped trying to encourage her to improve. Or that's how it seems to her.

But definitely she has loved. She has loved more deeply than anyone knows.

"You did know how to love and care," Marlene tells her, as if reading her thoughts. "And you can learn again. You *must* learn again. What is a mirror but a way to see yourself? Expect your first guide, when the bell tolls one."

"It won't toll. This is Christmas, and there was probably midnight mass, so it tolled at midnight."

"Go back to sleep, Keti."

And Marlene is gone.

Keti extinguishes the light and vows to leave it off if she awakens again. She only turned it on to look at the clock, because of the church bell, and to look at Marley.

She closes her eyes, sinking into the comfort of her warm bed, seeing in her mind the ice rink at Town Park.

***

The bell tolls again in the darkness. Marley barks twice, sharply, and Keti wakens and remembers her dream and Marlene's ghost, condemned to wander the world in Chanel and a pair of heels. She won't turn on her bedside lamp, but she's unable to resist glancing toward the mirror. It is glowing, glowing faintly but steadily, and Keti can see a figure there.

It looks like a child. But is it a child or someone extremely old and shrunken? It's hard to tell.

Keti squints through the darkness.

Marley growls.

"Who are you?" Keti whispers.

"The Ghost of Christmas Past—*your* past. Don't you know me, Keti?"

And Keti does. Right down to that face, with its odd features smoothed by Christmas or heaven or time. It's Edith Kitchen, who had been Keti White-chapel's best friend, her only real friend back then. Edith who'd died in the third grade. Edith who went through the ice and drowned. "Edith?"

"Yes. It's me. We're going to visit the past together, Keti. Come on."

It is a night of dreams, a night to dream. That's all Keti can think.

She holds on to Marley, uncertain.

"Your dog can come, too. If he will. We'll just be watching—come on." And a small child's arm extends from the mirror, the girl's hand reaching toward Keti.

Slowly, accepting the rules of the dream she can't stop, Keti climbs from the comfort of her bed. She wears silk pajamas in light blue, matching her eyes. "Come on, Marley. Edith's nice."

The dog jumps down from the bed and comes up to Keti's feet, leaning against her calves.

Keti reaches down to clasp Edith's hand.

It is warm and firm, and it casts Keti into the past.

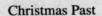

Christmas Past

Chapter 3

Bounty, Nevada
The Christmas Keti was seven

Santa Claus did not come to Keti's house. She never bothered explaining this to other people, and she wanted to smack Martin Collins just now for talking about the new skates Santa Claus had brought him. Keti's father gave her presents, yes, but not on Christmas Day, because Christmas reminded him of losing Keti's mother, and on Christmas he got drunk. He bought presents for Keti when he felt like it.

She loved nothing more than when her father took her somewhere and lifted her onto his shoulders. Like at the mine's Fourth of July company picnic. Times like that. Though he always said, *One of these days you're going to be too big for this, Keti*.

She was seven, and it worried her to be getting tall and too big to be lifted onto her father's shoulders.

Martin sat beside her on the bench at Town Park, his black hair sticking out in different directions, the way it always did, eyeing her curiously. "What did you get?" he asked.

It was morning, and according to the Town Hall clock, which she'd read on the way to the park, it was about nine. There weren't many people at the rink, just Keti and Martin, who was ten and the tallest person in his class, and Martin's younger sister, Bridget, who had also gotten new skates.

"That's rude," Keti told him. Martin Collins never talked to her at school, and Bridget, who was in Keti's class, was worse. Bridget looked like Snow White, with black hair and red lips. She was popular. She was friends with the girls who were meanest to Keti, the ones who made fun of her clothes.

"What's rude?" Martin asked.

He was so stupid, Keti couldn't believe it. Her skates—and by the way, no skates were going to make Martin a better skater than she was—were on. She stood up and stepped onto the ice, spinning before taking off to speed around the rink. Christmas didn't matter. Why did people get so thrilled over it?

Edith probably wouldn't come down to the rink for hours yet, she'd have so many presents to open. Her father was the mine manager, and they always had money. Keti's father made more money than Mr. Kitchen, according to him, but he spent more, too. Edith always gave Keti a Christmas present, the only one she'd get, and Keti had a present for Edith, a pink scarf she'd knitted at school, which was wrapped up and in the pocket of her coat.

"You're so stupid," Bridget told her brother. "You're the oldest, and you don't know *anything*."

"I'm a genius, handsome and charming," he said.

"Keti doesn't *get* Christmas presents. Her mother died on Christmas Day, and she doesn't get presents."

Martin sat on the bench, gazing at his new skates. There was so much information in what Bridget had just said. *Her mother died...* People did die. You didn't grow up in a mining town, with a father who worked in the mines, and not know that people died and that it could happen to you. He'd known Keti had no mother. That's why she was such a tomboy, everybody said. He'd never given her much thought.

But she didn't get presents?

And he'd said, *What did you get?*

Score one for Bridget. He had been stupid.

The solution was simple for him. He was the oldest, and his job was to help his mom take care of his brothers and sisters. So Keti would be an extra little sister. He would tell his parents, and they'd want to help her and make sure she got Christmas presents and other normal things, because that's how they were and that's how they'd taught their children to be. Every Christmas, each of his parents kept a secret from the other one. Separately, they would pick out someone in Bounty who needed something—money or a new coat or new books for the school. And then they would secretly give that present to the person they'd chosen, passing along the sales slip to the other parent on Christmas. Always in a specially decorated envelope. They loved to give, which they said was the only cure for sorrow.

Martin wasn't sure how they'd become this way, but he thought maybe it had to do with his brother dying years before. His brother Michael had died before Martin was born. He'd been six months old. Martin's parents said that Michael was an angel watching over all of them now.

He was actually, Martin knew, an archangel, a superpowerful angel.

Keti probably wouldn't *want* to be part of his family, though. That was the thing about her. She loved to act as if she was too good for everyone else because her father was the best "gyppo miner" at the Empress Mine. Gyp sheets were the forms that documented how much rock each miner moved. Gyppo miners got paid by how much they moved, and the sheets weren't confidential. *The competition,* Martin's father explained, *keeps everyone working as hard as they can.*

Sometimes so hard they made mistakes. His father had never said this to Martin, but Martin had overheard him saying it to other people.

Martin wondered if he would be able to enjoy skating on his new skates, now that he knew Keti never received Christmas presents. He decided he could live with it and skated out into the rink with Bridget. Homemade wooden hockey sticks leaned against the ticket shack—anyone could use them. Martin grabbed one, and Bridget grabbed another, but she was still learning to skate and she fell down. Martin set down his stick on the ice and helped his sister up, but then she said, "I'm *fine!*" and skated off.

Martin practiced with the stick, though they had no puck today. The pucks were kept inside, and the shack was closed because it was Christmas.

Keti yelled, "You're still slower than me."

"I'm not!"

They decided to race, from one end of the frozen pond to the other. Bridget said, "On your mark, ready, set, *go!*"

Martin stretched out his legs, which were longer than Keti's, but she just seemed to fly over the ice.

He didn't see exactly what happened, just caught her shape in her red pants and blue coat with the fur-fringed hood, as it went sailing, spinning, flat over the ice, skidding maybe twenty feet.

He slowed and circled back as Keti got up, her face a mess. It looked as if she had a bloody nose, and maybe she'd lost a tooth.

He skated toward her and asked, "Are you all right?"

But she just started skating away from him, and she reached the other end of the rink before she put her mittens up to her face, and he saw she was crying, too, although she tried not to show it.

He filled his mittened hands with snow and approached her. She'd chipped one of her front teeth, a permanent one just coming in—almost perpendicular to the way it should be—and her nose was bleeding.

"Sit down and put your head back," he said.

"I'm not sitting on the ice."

All thought of giving her a Christmas present disappeared. As soon as she stopped bleeding and crying, he was going to pull her hair and hit her with snowballs.

"You have to put your head back, to make your nose stop bleeding. And you chipped your tooth."

She climbed up onto the snowy bank and stood there, tilting her head back. "I won," she said. "New skates won't make you faster than me."

Martin felt bad that he was slower than a girl—and slower in his new skates. He was a good athlete; he was outdoors all the time, and he could hardly stand to be inside. He scooped up still more snow and hit her in the face with it.

Keti grabbed his coat and threw all her weight at him, knocking them both down in the snow.

"Martin Collins, I saw that!"

Keti sprang back from him, and Martin gaped at his aunt Bobbi, marching toward him.

Seeing Bobbi Kirk on her way over, Keti was sorry. She didn't want Martin to get into trouble and Bobbi was so snotty. She'd been homecoming queen years before, and no one was ever supposed to forget it. And she worked at the company store and was mean to Keti and Edith whenever they went in.

Keti said, "He didn't do anything! I fell down and got hurt. He's helping me."

Wobbling over on her new skates, Bridget chimed in, "That's right!"

Bobbi Kirk stopped, an expression of disbelief crossing her face. Letting out a snort of disgust, she said, "Right." Then, she came closer. "What happened, honey? Let me see."

By the time Keti sat in the Collinses' kitchen having hot chocolate, Martin had decided he didn't really want Keti Whitechapel as an adopted member of his family. She wasn't exactly an enemy, but he didn't have to love her, either. He could just wait patiently until she went home.

Bridget said, "Keti beat Martin in a race."

"I only tricked him," Keti said.

Bridget was in her class, and they weren't exactly friends, Martin knew. Still, Keti's answer surprised him, especially when she explained.

"I didn't really win. After I fell down I tricked him and kept skating. I had to trick him, because he's faster."

It was the second time she'd lied to help him out, Martin noticed, and this time he liked it less than he had the first time. "You are faster," he said and stood up. "You're the fastest skater in the whole school. It's not like it matters." And he left the noise in the kitchen and went into the living room where his dad was playing with his eighteen-month-old brother, George.

Martin sat on the floor and George wobbled toward him, saying, "Mar!" and Martin pulled him close and hugged him, and told himself that there were more important things than skating faster than a girl.

Chapter 4

Keti lets Edith lead her through the fog to the following year, when Keti is eight

Edith did not die on Christmas Day, but Keti remembered her death on the following Christmas Eve because she knew that among all the other things it meant there would be no gift from Edith. Edith, who was gone, Edith, who had been a misfit like Keti, and her only friend. Because Edith had had something wrong with her face. Keti had felt pretty beside Edith, and now she hated Christmas more than ever. Her father had gotten drunk the night before, and now he was asleep in his room in their cabin on Tomboy Road. No doubt he'd start drinking again as soon as he awoke.

Maybe she'd go sledding. She lived in the best place for sledding in all of Bounty. She could walk farther up Tomboy Hill, to the point that was the farthest from which anyone had ever sledded. But first of all someone needed to tamp down the snow to make it good for sleds, and she wasn't about to ask her father to do that today, not even if he was already awake. He would yell and throw things.

Keti's cat, Sam Cat, who was feral and would never let anyone hold her, jumped off the kitchen counter, where she'd been drinking milk out of Keti's cereal bowl. Keti knew she'd have to wash the dishes soon. Her father didn't wash dishes and he didn't cook. Most nights, they ate out at the diner or at the Miners' Boardinghouse. Keti made her own lunches for school.

Sam Cat yowled, and Keti heard someone out on the porch.

She went to the door.

Martin and Bridget Collins stood there. Martin was in the sixth grade now, and even taller than he used to be. All the girls in his class liked him, Bridget always said. His parents must have made him come to her house along with Bridget.

"What are you doing?" Keti said.

"You're to come home with us," Martin said.

"What do you mean?" She didn't ask them in. The house was dirty, and she didn't like people to visit. No one ever did anyway.

"We're to be together all through Christmas," Bridget said. "You're sleeping over."

"Why?" Keti demanded. The Collinses sometimes came across as do-gooders, and it was highly offensive to her to think that they might try to be doing good for the daughter of Luther Whitechapel.

"For fun. Our mom asked your dad yesterday. He said okay, but he probably forgot to tell you," Martin said.

All three of them translated "probably forgot to tell you" into "*got drunk* and forgot to tell you."

"I'm going sledding," Keti said. "I don't want to go to your house." She'd try to tamp down the snow herself so that her sled would run smoothly.

Martin watched her. She'd cut her blond hair as short as a boy's, and most of the time she dressed like a boy, too, the way she was today, in wool pants and a plain sweater. She still had the tooth she'd chipped the Christmas before. All her permanent teeth stuck out so far it was startling. If she were part of his family, Martin knew his parents would get her braces. He also knew that Luther Whitechapel would never bother to have Keti's teeth straightened, any more than he'd buy her nice clothes. No matter how good at sports Keti was, she'd be picked last for teams and made fun of always. And she wasn't about to accept the help of the Collins family. Martin looked at his sister and with his eyes conveyed what he could not say aloud: *I knew she was going to do this. I told you so.*

His mother had said, *Martin, you go with Bridget, and make sure Keti comes.*

But that was his job, given him by his mother, so somehow he had to accomplish it. It was that simple, even if he didn't like Keti Whitechapel; even if he'd rather not have her around his family's house on Christmas Day.

Keti's family had no Christmas tree. Neither did his—yet. They would go cut the tree once they were back with Keti.

It occurred to Martin that he might have the best luck if he was straightforward. He said, "We're supposed to go get our tree, and you're supposed to come."

"I'm not coming. You think I need to have Christmas, but I don't. I don't *like* Christmas."

"We have presents for you," he said, which was true.

She gave him a long-suffering look, then shrugged. "Okay."

"And bring your pajamas and stuff," Bridget said, "because you're sleeping over." As if she hadn't looked at her mother with horror initially and said, *I don't want to have her over. People will think we're friends!*

* * *

"Keti, I'm so glad you're here." Mrs. Collins wrapped her arms around Keti and pulled her close.

Keti submitted to being hugged but said nothing. The Collinses were being *charitable.* She knew this and she didn't like being the object of their charity. After all, her dad wasn't poor. He just didn't like Christmas. And the Collins family had five kids already. *They* weren't rich.

"Would you like some pumpkin pie?" Mrs. Collins offered. "Everyone's allowed a piece to tide them over while they go cut the tree."

"Yes, please," Keti answered.

"I do feel bad for the Kitchens," Mrs. Collins said to her husband, Charles, as she sliced a piece of pie and served it to Keti on turquoise Fiesta Dinnerware. "I took them cookies, but it's so sad over there. Edith was their only child."

Keti sat at the Collinses' big table. It was nicer than her father's table. It was made of a light-colored wood and was big enough for their entire family. They had another table in their dining room, too. If Keti's mother had lived, she and her family might have had tables like this. But it was just Keti and her father, so there was no need for anything fancy.

Martin said, "We could go sing Christmas carols to them."

Keti wondered how Edith's parents would feel about having someone sing carols to them. Probably all they wanted was to have Edith back. She felt that way, too. She told Martin, "They just want Edith. Don't be stupid."

She knew, the moment she said it, that at the Collins house people would think this was really impolite, calling one of the family stupid. "Sorry," she muttered.

"That's a nice idea, Martin," said Mrs. Collins.

"Keti's probably right," he said, and he left the room.

"It wasn't a bad idea," Keti said belatedly, trying to make up for her mistake. She finished her pie quickly and took her plate to the sink and rinsed it. Mrs. Collins complimented her on her nice manners, and then Keti went to find Martin. He was sitting on the floor in the den near a space that had been cleared for the tree, helping George put rings over a rocking pillar. It was a PlaySkool toy like the one Keti had played with when she was little.

She said, "We could go caroling."

"We have to get the tree," he said, "and then I help Dad put the lights on it."

Well, la-di-da, Keti almost said.

"Just offering," she told him instead.

The phone rang. "Charles!" Mrs. Collins called, and Martin's father hurried through the den to the kitchen.

A moment later, they heard Mr. Collins saying something about the mine. He was an engineer, and he was going to have to go to work to take care of a ventilation problem. "But the tree!" howled Martin's sister Amy from the kitchen.

It was obvious, suddenly, that the Collins family wasn't going to have a perfect Christmas after all.

Martin had the idea. He had it because he'd learned, in his family, that the only way to really make yourself feel good when you felt rotten was to help someone else. The Kitchens, Edith's parents, probably felt more rotten than he did, than anyone else did this Christmas.

"What are you doing?" said his mother as he began looking up the number in the phone book.

"I'm going to ask Mr. Kitchen if he'll help us get our Christmas tree."

Keti, who had picked up George and followed Martin to the phone, watched his mother's expression. She looked stunned. As if she didn't know what to say.

"He'll be at the mine, won't he?" Mrs. Collins finally pointed out.

"Nope, he's on the owl shift."

She washed her hands at the sink.

Martin was aware of his mother and Keti listening as Mrs. Kitchen answered the phone, saying, "Hello?"

"Mrs. Kitchen, this is Martin Collins. Is Mr. Kitchen there?"

"Yes. Yes, he is. One moment." At Edith's burial almost a year ago, people had said, Mrs. Kitchen hadn't wanted them to lower the coffin. She'd been on her hands and knees sobbing. Martin thought about this while he waited for Mr. Kitchen to come to the phone.

"Hello." He had one of those warm, deep voices. Martin had always liked him.

"Mr. Kitchen, this is Martin Collins," he began. "My dad had to go down in the mine, and we haven't got our tree yet. I thought of you, because I know you already did your shift…"

Mr. Kitchen interrupted. "Kathleen and I will be glad to help you get that tree. As long as we have some assistance. You and some of your brothers and sisters, maybe."

Keti was really glad to see Mr. and Mrs. Kitchen, who hugged her and told her how they'd missed her. Not all of the Collins kids came; not all of them had wanted to. Bridget had chosen to stay home with four-year-old Paul and two-and-a-half-year-old George. Keti thought Bridget was afraid to talk to the Kitchens because of Edith's being dead.

It was nice of the Kitchens to take the Collins

family to get their tree, Keti thought. Funny, the Kitchens seemed almost *happy* to be helping. They definitely seemed happy to see her.

Amy Collins, who was ten, appointed herself the expert and chose what she considered the perfect tree. It was in the Bridalveil area. Mr. Kitchen and Martin took turns with the saw, cutting it down. As he was sawing, Martin smelled the sap and the needles. He wanted to see the rings on the trunk and count them, because they would tell him how old the tree was.

Behind him, Keti and Amy stamped their feet to keep warm and Mrs. Kitchen warned her husband and Martin to be careful.

The tree toppled over in the snow.

Martin crouched by the trunk and counted rings. Keti said, "What are you doing?"

"Finding out how old it is. Twenty-one!" he concluded. "It's twenty-one years old."

"And now its life is over," Keti said matter-of-factly. The others were already dragging the tree to the Kitchens' station wagon, and Keti ran to help.

Martin thought about what she'd said, and he took off a glove to touch the stump of the tree, and then he picked up some snow and gazed at that. He couldn't imagine anywhere he'd rather be than outside among all the trees.

Back in the fog with Edith

The fifty-five-year-old Keti wonders why Edith showed her that particular Christmas when she was eight. And Edith *didn't* show her any presents. But Keti, being there, locked in the memory, remembered she had felt *wanted.* Wanted by the Collins family, and wanted by the Kitchens. People wanted her around.

Which proved what Keti had always believed, that she'd had a perfectly good childhood.

The dog, Marley, beside her, leans against her leg as Keti finds herself on a sidewalk, on Bounty's Main Street. She sees groups of teenagers walking past, laughing.

She knows Martin by his shape. He's tall, broad shouldered, handsome in an unusual way. She can see the bones in his face, the perfect bones. All the girls like him. He's one of the brighter kids who'll soon be graduating from Bounty High School.

Fifteen-year-old Keti saw Martin Collins ahead. It was Noel Night in Bounty. On Noel Night, the teenagers all met at the Town Hall to receive gifts from their Secret Santas. Keti was Secret Santa to a boy named Russell Logan, and she found it embarrassing. No other word for it.

It wasn't just that he was poor. Everyone in Bounty was kind of poor.

It wasn't even that he wore glasses.

It was things like the way he talked. He couldn't use words with fewer than three syllables.

Tonight, he would find out that she, Keti White-chapel, was his Secret Santa. She would be nice to him—kind of. She'd learned to get by in life with *nice*.

"Keti! Keti, my girl!"

It was her father, coming out of one of Bounty's two bars. This one was The Underground. A man was with him. He looked vaguely familiar to Keti, and Keti had a bad feeling about him.

"Do you know Roy Knott, Keti?"

One of the miners.

"He's signed on at the mine, and he's going to be living with us. Someone else to wash the dishes, eh, Keti?"

Keti didn't believe for a second that this other miner would wash a single plate at their house. He'd just get drunk with her father.

Roy Knott was tall, like her father, and thin and a bit hunched over. Keti supposed he was around thirty-five, but already he'd lost most of his hair. Her father had a full head of hair.

"You look pretty, Keti," Roy said.

She was breathing steam in the cold air, but the breath of the two men was foul. Roy Knott had been drinking rum, and Keti detested that smell. She was sure that she didn't look pretty. No one ever called her pretty, because of her teeth. She'd heard some of the guys at school talking, saying Keti Whitechapel would be okay if they could just stick someone else's face on her body.

She didn't even bother to say, "Thank you," to Roy Knott's patent insincerity.

Roy asked, "You got a boyfriend?"

"Keti's got loads of boyfriends," interjected her father.

This was demeaning. She didn't *need* boyfriends, and she sure didn't have any. Girls who looked like her never had boyfriends. Or friends of any kind, for that matter.

"Anything special you want for Christmas, Keti?" the man asked.

Her father said nothing, as if they had Christmas like other people.

Keti shrugged.

"How about a pretty sweater?" asked Roy. "You'd like that, wouldn't you?" He leered at her breasts.

Keti didn't answer. The *only* thing she wanted was to have her teeth straightened. She didn't mind the one chipped one, but she did mind all her teeth sticking out too far. There was an orthodontist in Bounty, now that it was no longer just a company town. People were talking about developing a ski area here.

All Keti could think about was money, wanting money to get her teeth fixed. She'd asked her dad about the orthodontist, and he'd told her she looked fine as she was. Which clearly meant he wasn't going to spring for it.

She was glad to get away from her father and his friend, who was going to live with them so that she'd have *two* drunken miners at home instead of just one. She continued to Town Hall, dreading her encounter with Russell Logan. Of course, she'd put her name on his present. Although she didn't like him, she'd given him something she thought he'd like. It was a special pencil case that was also a slide rule, because he was so brainy.

In the vast Town Hall, she looked around, thinking about Martin Collins and the reality that only the prettiest girls could get his attention. She would probably go to the Collins house again this Christmas Eve, as she always did. But she would mostly spend time with Amy, not with Martin—or Bridget, for that matter. Bridget acted as if she was too good for the rest of the world. In any case, Martin Collins would never notice Keti the way she wanted him to notice her. Because that was how things were. She looked the way she looked, and someday she might get to go on a date with some boy who had the sex appeal of Russell Logan—or someone who'd made a bet with his friends that she would let him touch her breasts. She'd heard that idea being whispered about, too.

She went over to the big tree to look for a package

with her name on it. Her Secret Santa had been especially nice this year. There had been a poem by Robert Frost in her locker and new laces for her ice skates outside her front door one morning. There had been many more small surprises for her than she'd ever gotten before from a Secret Santa.

She finally found a box with her name on it under the tree. It was small, like a jewelry box, wrapped in green paper. Keti opened the paper carefully, then lifted the lid on the box. There was the card, and it said, "Sincerely, Martin Collins, your Secret Santa." When she lifted the card, she found a necklace beneath. From a silver chain hung a crystal snowflake.

Keti peered around Town Hall, and she saw Martin by himself looking out the window at the Christmas lights on the street below. Two girls in Amy Collins's class, two years below Martin's, were looking at him and whispering and giggling.

Hoping.

Keti put on the necklace, and then she walked over to him. No need to be afraid, because he didn't like her the way she wanted, would never like her that way. He'd been such a nice Secret Santa for reasons that had nothing to do with her. He was just nice to people, as if it was his profession.

Tonight, Keti was wearing the white sweater with the navy-blue Fair Isle pattern around the neck that

Mrs. Collins had knitted for her the year before, and with it she wore her black stretch ski pants.

She tapped Martin's back and he spun around.

She held out the snowflake, to show him she was wearing it. "Thanks! You were a really good Santa." She smiled with her lips closed over her teeth, the way she always did.

His brown eyes saw the snowflake, and he reached out and gave her a hug. Then, he let go. "Merry Christmas, Keti."

The same Christmas, on through the fog

The warmth fades in the chill of fog. Keti's cheeks, which have been so warm, suddenly react to the frigid night and she is apprehensive. She remembers the rest of that Christmas season. Detestable Roy Knott moving in, and the two men being drunk all the time. Then her father throwing Roy out, finally, just after New Year's, because Roy had tried to get fresh with Keti.

And the things Roy had shouted… "You may as well let me, Luther. Nobody's going to want to look at her face."

"The past isn't always happy," says Edith now. Edith, who—if she'd lived—could have written a book about the cruel things people say on the subject of imperfect faces. "But it doesn't have to ruin us."

The Christmas Eve when Keti was sixteen

Keti's father was dead. He had died nine days earlier, when a slab broke loose overhead and fell on him and his partner, Hoss Skelling. Hoss's legs had been crushed. Luther Whitechapel had died instantly.

At the Catholic church and also after the funeral, there had been discussions about what was to be done with Keti. Keti had overheard snatches of the talk. As far as she was concerned, she was old enough to live on her own and that was what she intended to do. But Mr. Collins had insisted, "She has to finish school!" as if anything other than that would be shocking.

Keti would get a job, she thought. She could work in the mine offices. She could even work below, as some other women in Bounty did, a few of them.

Now the Collinses were expecting her for Christmas Eve, but she didn't want to go. They would want her to live with them. No, they would *ask* her to live with them, even though they didn't really want her there. They would ask her because that was the kind of people they were.

So it was Christmas Eve, and for once no one was drunk in her father's house, because now her father was gone forever. This was her house, or at least it would be, people had said, once everything was settled. Her father hadn't ever made a will, and that bothered

Keti—she'd heard rumors that it would all belong to the state. But no one was kicking her out just yet.

There were heavy feet on the porch outside, and faces peered in the window.

Keti wished she were invisible. The Collinses. The Collinses had come to the door—that had been Bridget and Martin peering in, and they had seen her. Martin, who was home from college. Martin was going to be a physician. He wanted to help people.

"Keti, come out!" called Bridget, who, this past year, had learned to at least *act* friendly, some of the time, if none of her friends—the popular crowd—were around. Bridget tried the front door, then knocked. "Keti, it's Bridg. Let me in."

Irritated, dressed in some baggy corduroys and a huge sweatshirt she'd rescued from the Bounty free box, where people left things they didn't need anymore, Keti yanked the door open.

Bridget smiled, and her brother, behind her, did the same. "C'mon. Come over. Look…Martin's home."

"She can see that," Martin pointed out.

Bridget ignored him. Keti looked at Bridget's black curls, at her fresh complexion and white teeth, at her Snow White prettiness, which had only increased through the years. Everyone said Bridget would be queen of the junior prom this year.

Keti saw Bridget peering past her and was glad that she herself always kept the house clean, at least.

My house, now. The thought didn't make her happy, the way she would have wanted it to.

To stop Bridget from peering around her into the house, Keti said, "All *right.* I'm coming."

Martin, who hadn't looked inside or at her and still did not, said, "Good," and turned away, swinging his car keys.

Keti was in the Collinses master bedroom, sitting on the huge bed, where Mrs. Collins had asked her to sit. "Keti, we want you to come and live with us. You're like a part of our family, and we hate the idea of you living alone."

Keti almost told Mrs. Collins that she absolutely was *not* part of the Collins family, but that would have been rude. And Mrs. Collins was nice. She wasn't insincere, not exactly. Though Keti knew darned well that she wasn't the same to Mr. or Mrs. Collins as their own kids were.

Keti said, "I'll be fine."

"It's not good for you to be alone, and, honey, I don't know what they're going to do about the house."

They didn't have to be defined. Keti didn't know who *they* were, only that her father might not have paid his taxes or might owe money to someone, or the "estate"—which sounded like wealth, but wasn't, necessarily—could take years to "straighten out."

"I'm going to work in the mine," she announced. "Mr. Spencer said he'd hire me in the new year."

Mrs. Collins looked at her in horror. "Not *in* the mine, surely. In the office, though…"

"In the mine," Keti interrupted. "Some women do." And the men didn't like it and never would. But they'd accept Keti faster than many other women. Her dad had been the best miner in Bounty, and so they would be glad to give her a chance down below.

Well, not glad. But they wouldn't be so hard on her. Most of them had known her for her whole life.

"Keti, Mr. Collins and I would like to see you finish school, and we know your dad would have wanted that, too."

Well, that was an interesting thought, but Keti didn't buy it. Her father hadn't cared much what she did, short of something immoral. He'd had no ideas about her "finishing school."

"Please come and live with us. We want you to be our girl, Keti," Mrs. Collins said.

Keti did know something about the Collins family, though, and about Mr. and Mrs. Collins. If she, Keti Whitechapel, came to live with them, Mr. and Mrs. Collins would treat her exactly the same as they did their other children. It would be a matter of honor with them. They would buy her the same clothes they bought Bridget or Amy. They would make her do her homework the same way.

Keti wasn't sure she wanted that. It had occurred to her that maybe, if somehow her father *did* have some money set by, she could have a few things she'd never had before. But it was more important to hang on to the house, if that was possible, and to live frugally. That was how she'd always lived.

"I'm fine," Keti repeated. "I'll be fine."

"But, Keti, honey, I don't think they'll let you stay in the house."

They. They. Keti didn't even want to know who *they* were. "I think they will," she insisted.

Just before noon, the front doorbell chimed. The Collinses' bell played a song. Keti heard a voice outside speaking low, and then the muffled sound of an argument from the front entryway.

She followed the noises uneasily and saw a man and a woman standing near the door. They were elegantly dressed, and they were not from Bounty. Keti didn't recognize them.

Mr. Collins showed them into the living room, closing the door behind. Keti sensed something in his eyes, something cool and decisive. Martin's father seemed in charge of everything in the world just then.

He did not like these out-of-town people, Keti knew that.

But Mrs. Collins said, "Keti? Keti, these are relatives of yours."

Keti liked the look of the woman, who wore an elegant red suit that fit so perfectly that it must have been made specifically for her. She was blond, perhaps Keti's father's age—definitely older than Mrs. Collins.

"Keti, I'm your aunt Marlene. Great-aunt, really, but I think we'll let it go with *aunt*. I was your daddy's mother's youngest sister. And this is my husband, Edward."

Keti decided that it was at least partly Edward that Mr. Collins didn't like. Edward had a clipped mustache and his black hair was combed back, and he was extremely handsome—like a movie star. Not young, though, more like, well, Clark Gable or someone like that. His suit looked expensive, too. It was black with tiny pale grey stripes, and his shoes shone. No, these people were not from Bounty.

"We thought Keti could stay with us," Mrs. Collins told their visitors. "That way she can finish school here in Bounty, where her friends are."

Friends? Keti thought. That was a laugh.

Edward was giving her an appraising look through narrowed eyes, and Keti imagined she could read his thoughts—which were about her teeth and her corduroys and sweatshirt. She knew he was thinking that she wasn't much to look at.

"Would you like to come home with us, Keti?" asked the pretty older blond woman, the woman who did seem too young to be a *great*-aunt.

Edward's eyes slid sideways toward Marlene with a look that said they might as well leave Keti where she was.

Then Martin came into the front hall. He looked at Keti's aunt Marlene and at her husband. His expression was almost rude. He seemed to have the gist of the conversation right away, and then his eyes swept over Aunt Marlene more carefully, and there was nothing friendly in his look. *He* didn't look impressed by her clothes. "You're from Las Vegas," he said.

Las Vegas. Keti's mind filled with the thought of it. The city. She could live in a real city.

Edward's head lifted slightly, and he seemed to gain height, though he was shorter than Martin. Well, most people were. "I don't think you have any part in this discussion, son," he said, and there was something unkind in his tone, something mocking, that clearly implied Martin was *not* an adult.

Although Martin was.

Keti did not understand. But suddenly she wasn't sure she wanted to go with Aunt Marlene and Edward. Edward, she could tell, was cruel.

"I don't think anyone in Bounty is likely to let you take Keti," Martin said matter-of-factly, sounding as if he knew Edward, which couldn't be possible.

"Martin," exclaimed his mother. "These are Keti's relatives."

"So?" Martin said.

Mr. Collins gave his eldest a look that unmistakably said, *That's enough from you.*

Martin ran his tongue along the inside of his cheek.

Mystified, Keti allowed herself a look at Martin. She could still observe him, even if she tried to talk to him as little as possible. She never wanted him looking at her. He was beautiful, whereas she was ugly. Down in the Empress Tunnel was the place for her, where the grime, the dust of the hard rock would settle on her.

Martin did not like Edward. *Seriously* did not like Edward. And the thought of going with the man, even with nice Aunt Marlene, chilled Keti.

"Keti, why don't you at least come out to brunch with us," Aunt Marlene said. "We just wanted to start that way, because we know it's scary to go live with people you've never met before. We can tell you all about our house in Las Vegas. We have a swimming pool, you know."

"Would you like to go to brunch with them, Keti?" Mrs. Collins asked, though neither her husband nor Martin appeared to think much of the idea.

"Yes," Keti said. "Let me just…get my parka."

"Right," Martin said, grabbing her hand and pulling her into the next room.

Martin Collins, holding her hand.

He dropped it in the living room. Keti gave him a perplexed look and picked up her parka, glancing at her pile of gifts, which was the same size as that of any other member of the family. There was the box that contained her new sweater from the Collinses and the blue stuffed dog, a present from Martin like the dogs he'd given his sisters, on top of it. Amy had gotten a white dog, and Bridget's was pink.

He hissed, so as not to be overheard, "Keti, don't go with them."

"Why not?"

"I mean to Las Vegas. Go to breakfast, if you want, but don't leave Bounty with them."

Keti blinked at him once, then looked away. Why should any man look so good that it hurt her eyes to see him. He didn't have a narrow face, yet its bones seemed impossibly fine where they could be seen beneath his skin. And that cleft in his chin. Amy Collins, Amy, who was Keti's friend in a way Bridget never would be, always told Keti about her classmates making idiots of themselves over Martin. Amy could do a great impression of the homecoming queen tripping and making her breasts almost tumble out of her bra at the sight of Martin. Keti liked Amy.

"Why not?" Keti repeated. "What do you know about them?"

Martin gave her a pointed look and said, in an

undertone that also conveyed his opinion regarding her naïveté, "Can you say *pimp?*"

Keti's jaw dropped so that she forgot, for a second, about covering her teeth with her lips. She promptly caught herself, but still she had to ask, "How do you know?"

He wasn't abashed. "I know. Let's put it that way."

He was looking at her the same way he looked at Amy or Bridget when they were being stupid. Just the same way. Like a sister.

I don't want to be his sister.

"*How* do you know?" she repeated.

His eyes changed. Not much. But enough.

Enough so that she knew all at once, or maybe she simply *hoped,* or had the courage to dream suddenly, that Martin Collins also perceived that she had qualities that would be intriguing to a pimp.

That was news to Keti Whitechapel, but she wasn't going to think too much about it. All she knew was that, if she lived with the Collins family, Martin would come home sometimes from college, and she would be here.

She felt faint.

Apparently deciding he'd gotten through to Keti, Martin smiled, and his smile was just a little chilly, indicating that he didn't think the idea of her going to live with a pimp and his wife—*were* these two really married?—was a reason to smile.

"There aren't pimps in Nevada," Keti told him. "There are brothels, but there aren't pimps."

Martin's unblinking expression conveyed his mesmerized disbelief that there could be a sixteen-year-old girl anywhere who didn't know that, yes, there were pimps in the State of Nevada.

"Keti, darling?"

It was Mrs. Collins.

"Are you ready to go with your aunt and uncle, sweetheart? Now, you're just going for brunch. They're going to take you to the Grand Imperial." The only place in Bounty that served Sunday brunch—or any meal at all on Christmas Day.

Keti nodded.

"And you're to come back here afterward," she said firmly, as if she was responsible for Keti. Mrs. Collins glowered at her oldest son, with a look that said she certainly hoped he hadn't been speaking to Keti of things no son of hers should know about.

The car they drove was a Thunderbird, with whitewall tires. Edward didn't open the door for Keti, even after Aunt Marlene gave him a look clearly encouraging him to do so.

Keti opened her door for herself, thinking of what she knew about Nevada's legal brothels—there were two just outside the Bounty city limits—and of what on earth a pimp might do. Did pimps *run* brothels? In the backseat, she turned over the things everyone had said to her. The swimming pool and the *money* and Aunt Marlene's friendly smile and her obvious desire to have Keti with her.

And then that interesting conversation with Martin Collins.

At the Grand Imperial, as the three of them waited to be seated, Edward twirled his car keys and looked at the hostess and at every other woman in the place. Not the way the boys Keti knew looked at girls— even, sometimes, at Keti, though only at her body, and never at her face. Edward didn't look at women as if he wanted to, well, *do* things with them.

His expression reminded her more of the way her father's face had looked when he'd been considering the purchase of a new drill at the hardware store. Thoughtful. Practical. Assessing.

The women were...*merchandise*. Keti realized this with a mixture of shock and, well, admiration. This Edward wasn't one to get silly about anything. Clearly, he was sensible about money.

But he was a little scary, as well.

And Martin Collins had probably given her good advice when he'd urged her not to go with them. Not yet, anyhow.

At the table in the hotel dining room, where Keti had never eaten in her entire life, Aunt Marlene assured her she could order anything she wanted. Aunt Marlene treated Keti as if she were younger than sixteen, but Keti didn't really mind. And surely Aunt Marlene wouldn't let Edward the Pimp do anything to her or with her.

"You could have your own room," Aunt Marlene told her. "I understand if you don't want to decide yet, Keti. But you're my only blood relative, now your father's gone."

"How come I've never met you till now?" Keti asked, finding it was possible to look straight at the other woman. When she did, she knew that she *was* looking into the face of a blood relation. Except that Marlene was so pretty. And Keti never had been and never would be.

Edward gave a twisted little smile that betrayed worldly cynicism and also amusement—the way Martin Collins had been smiling not too long before, Keti reflected. "Tell her, dear," he urged Marlene, in a way that was definitely unpleasant.

He's mean, Keti thought.

But Marlene seemed impervious to Edward's disdain. "Honey, your father didn't approve of me. He told me never to come around, and you may as well know that right now."

Keti couldn't bring herself to say, *Why not?*

If Edward was a pimp, was Marlene a prostitute? Keti doubted that. Marlene was refined, classy.

"You see, I own some brothels, and that didn't sit right with your father. It may not sit right with you, either, but there's no use in pretending I'm anything but what I am," Marlene said.

She seemed to feel no shame in the admission. *And why should she?* Keti shocked herself by thinking. It was just a way to make a living. And Keti had understood the importance of having money often enough in her own life to have few scruples about how people chose to earn it. Clearly, Aunt Marlene was good at what she did.

But I can't be part of that, she thought.

People would be scandalized.

Martin Collins wouldn't like her.

What makes you think he ever will, Keti White-chapel?

She was like a sister to Martin. No more, no less.

But for some reason, Keti was keen not to lose his respect. She said, "I think for now, I should live with the Collinses." Then, because Marlene looked disappointed, she added, "Just, maybe, until I finish school. Bounty's always been my home." There were still pinpricks of sadness in Marlene's eyes, however, and Keti *needed* to make those go away. "Will you come and see me again?"

"Yes, Keti." Aunt Marlene completely ignored Edward's smirks. She leaned forward and kissed Keti's cheek. "I certainly will."

Chapter 5

A different world, six Christmases later

When the fog swirls away again, Keti sees lights. Unexpectedly, they are the lights outside the Empress Mine, tall bright lamps that illuminate the gravel-and-dirt parking area in the winter evening.

"I don't want to see this," she tells Edith. "I don't want to see any more." Her memories of working in the Empress Tunnel are in some ways happy. But she remembers keenly and with some bittersweetness the one Christmas Eve when she was on shift at the mine.

Edith says, "What are you afraid to see here?"

"Nothing. And it's not *fear,* anyhow. I just don't want to look back. I always look ahead."

"If you truly looked forward," Edith says, "truly saw the future you are creating, we wouldn't be doing this, looking back at Christmases past."

Keti ponders the statement, wondering what it could mean. *I do look ahead. I'm an expert at looking ahead, and that's why I'll never be poor again.*

She crouches down on the sidewalk in her nightgown and wraps her arms around Marley. She doesn't want to see, doesn't want to remember these times that are gone, because they *are* gone. And she can't bring them back.

Even using earplugs, Keti always experienced the noise within the Empress Tunnel as completely deafening. The drilling, the loaders, the many machines, huge and small, that brought ore out of this tunnel to be processed.

Her shift was almost over. She stepped near the rib and lifted up a long pole to knock free a small slab from the roof. Then she approached the face again, taking up the drill, whose power shook her entire body. She made sport of drilling as fast and well as a man, as well as her father would have drilled.

Marlene, of course, told her she didn't need to work down here. She was willing to lend Keti money to start a business of her own. But Keti was leery of borrowing from anyone, for any reason. At the age of seventeen she'd found she actually had some money, after the settling of her father's estate. A court-appointed trustee oversaw her small inheritance until she was eighteen. Keti spent as little of it as possible, and she hung on to her father's house, continuing to live in it. People loved the little ski resort that had opened in Bounty. This wasn't a bad place to own a house, especially since she could add to her modest pile of wealth by working in the mine.

The only money she'd spent had gone to the orthodontist. The Collinses had offered to pay, almost insisted upon it. But Keti had refused to take from them what her father, she'd believed, had been able to afford. And when the inherited money was hers, when she found she had enough, she used a portion of that each month. Three years of braces, and then another year with a retainer day and night. But now, at twenty-two, she had straight teeth, although one of them was still chipped.

Now, she was considered good-looking. The men of the Empress Mine gave her a hard time; she was a woman, they were miners, and though this wasn't as bad a mine to work as some, Keti put up with a certain amount of crudity.

Her arms trembled with the force of the drill, and

she thought of what Marlene had said to her. *You'll ruin your lungs working down there, girl. Silicosis. Isn't that what all the hard-rock miners get?*

Keti's partner, a guy her own age named Dylan, set the charges.

Blasts of the whistle, and they headed for the mantrip, to be out of the mine when the charges went off. For Keti, it was the end of the shift, and the cage took her up, up, up, with fellow workers; two out of the other fourteen were women. She nodded at Debbie Wilson and Mandy Skiff. When the cage rattled to a stop after a slowish ascent—not the eight hundred feet per minute of the descent—she followed them to the big doors leading out of the mine, heading for the women's dry room.

Lucille Harold was already there, and she said, "There's a man waiting for you, Keti."

"For me?" She couldn't imagine who that would be. There were no men in her life—not in the way Lucille's expression seemed to imply. Men did occasionally ask her out, and sometimes she went, and she'd had a boyfriend for a while and done what he wanted, but she hadn't liked it much and had broken up with him soon afterward. She'd thought sex should be something… Well, a little mysterious and transcendent and beautiful. And her couple of experiences with the miner who had finally gone to work in Montana had been prosaic and disappointing.

She showered, scrubbing hard. It was Christmas Eve, and she would be both welcome and expected at the Collins house. Aunt Marlene had invited her to Las Vegas, but Martin was supposed to be coming home. Home from Vietnam.

She connected the "man" waiting for her with Martin Collins. Could it be him? It wouldn't be Mr. Collins, not the way Lucille had referred to the person who was waiting. She hurried out of the shower, hoping to ask Lucille for more details, but her coworker was gone. She caught Debbie, a thirty-five-year-old former barmaid, who'd discovered how much more money she could make mining. "Did Lucille say anything about what this guy looked like?"

Debbie shook her head and ran a brush through her hair before pulling on a red parka. "What are you doing tonight?" she asked Keti.

"Oh, I have somewhere to go," Keti said, feeling grateful for the fact. It couldn't be Martin outside. He'd have no reason to meet her at the tunnel.

Martin Collins stood in the falling snow just outside the entrance to the mine. Amy had written to him that Keti was working here, and someone inside had just confirmed that she was on the job and that her shift was about to end.

The snow was cold and clean, so unlike all the

horror, the messiness in the country. He had been an idiot patriotic kid, wanting to do the all-American thing, the old-fashioned thing, the traditional thing.

He'd *enlisted*. He'd decided, halfway through medical school, to enlist. To go to Vietnam.

It had been the stupidest thing he'd ever done. But at the same time it *hadn't* been a mistake. A wound had shifted him from *that* world, too, in spite of everything, a beautiful land and a place where he'd received more medical training, irreplaceable experience. Where he'd begun to live on adrenaline and fear and the strange high that came from functioning superbly in terrifying situations. His injuries had brought him to Walter Reed Army Medical Center, and he'd spent two months there. Members of his family had come from Nevada to Washington, D.C., to be close to him, but then he'd eluded them, too.

Now he stood in the gravel parking lot feeling that cold, clean snow falling on his hair and face. He was in Bounty. He was here.

But he wasn't ready to go home quite yet.

And so he'd turned his secondhand Mustang toward the Empress Tunnel on a whim. Miners worked all hours. The mine might even remain open Christmas Day. Some people worked holidays—for instance, the prostitutes at the line of legal brothels just outside the Bounty city limits. That line had grown, too, now supporting three such establishments. Martin hadn't stopped. He had seen more of the world in Vietnam, too much for comfort, but he wanted to shut the ugliness out. He wanted the purity and simplicity of the mountains, of his hometown.

But he wasn't quite ready to return to his childhood home, nor to see his family. They wouldn't really know him, not who he was now, and he couldn't *make* them know him.

He was outside and he liked that, liked the wide Nevada sky, liked the brisk, thin air.

Martin watched one woman leave the mine, but it was someone with dark hair. Why did he want to see Keti? Maybe because she was part of his family and yet not part of it, exactly how he saw himself now. He watched the woman miner. He had known women while he was away. He remembered them with sadness and wondered if his whole life would now be tinged with sadness and rage, if that was all he'd brought back from Vietnam.

Except, of course, his wound.

And that was healed.

She appeared, then, exiting from the mine, and he knew her at once. Her parka was light blue, and she wore a matching ski hat. He recognized her slim hips, her lean yet voluptuous body. She looked both ways in the parking lot, then spotted him and strode toward him, that loping, floating walk.

Keti—and yet not Keti.

The face he remembered had become streamlined. With her teeth fixed—all but the chipped tooth—she resembled Grace Kelly. The teeth had been such a distraction, always drawing the eyes away from her other features. Her hair was the white-blond of a Norse goddess, and her mouth was sensitive-looking, mobile, unexpected.

He noticed a tingling throughout his body. Why shouldn't he, even if this was the first time he'd felt this...since? Yes, his wound had healed, physically.

But something had happened to his mind, something that made sex seem so trivial that arousal could no longer happen automatically, by reflex. And this was no simple reflex, more like something he'd awaited, awaited his whole life.

I should be home already, he thought. *Instead I've been lurking outside the mine, waiting for her to emerge.*

Now, he would have to go to the house. And confront his mother's tremulous face, his father's quiet solemnity. Their relief that he *hadn't* been killed in a foreign jungle, tending fallen comrades, fallen friends, some friends he hadn't been able to tend, to reach, to help or save. Now his family would want to help him, and none of them—not his brothers or sisters or either of his parents—would have the slightest idea of what to say or how to look.

If only he could be alone here in these mountains. But Bounty wasn't that kind of place. For now, the one person he could face was Keti Whitechapel.

Martin looked so different, it frightened her.

His hair was too long, dark, almost black, and wavy. His brown eyes—the change was most dramatic there, she thought. He wore an olive drab parka over an old olive shirt—fatigues—and underneath that, a long-sleeved T-shirt and jeans.

But he was still handsome, his face still chiseled, that cleft in his chin still so appealing, so that she longed to touch it.

And she felt a rush through her whole body.

He's like your brother, Keti, and that's all you are to him—a kind of sister.

She strove to be sisterly. After all, it wasn't as if she had too much experience being anything other than sisterly. "Are you all right? Of course, you're not." He'd left medical school and enlisted. People in Bounty had respected him for this. They had all been proud.

And then he'd been wounded.

A groin wound, Amy's letter had said. Underlined.

But Amy had also confided that her brother had somehow come through with "everything intact." Now, he was out of the hospital. He was here.

And his groin was none of her business.

She stood close to him in the falling snow. If things had been different, if he hadn't so obviously been *through* something, she would have backed far away. She wanted only to comfort him now. "How long have you been home? I can't believe they let you come out for a walk so soon after you got back."

"I haven't been home yet."

Something strummed through Keti as she digested this bit of information. *He came to see me.* But it was more than that. She understood at once that he didn't want to go home; even if home was probably the best place for him. There was a shakiness to him, but he didn't appear to be on drugs. Undoubtedly he'd seen—and perhaps done—terrible things. But his family loved him, and they *would* help.

"I thought," he said, "I'd see what you were doing."

Getting off work, Keti almost said. *Obviously.*

"Living in my dad's old house." She shrugged. "I'm doing all right." She was talking about how she was doing financially, but she realized as she spoke that it wouldn't occur to him to think about how she was getting on in terms of money. He wasn't wired that way.

She didn't know what to say about Vietnam, whether or not to mention it. But she thought if she could say the *right* thing, that would be best, so she tried. "Are you having culture shock, being back here?"

He shook his head. "It's not that. But it's not the same here. It's different from what it used to be."

The snow fell over and between them as Keti watched Martin and waited.

"I'd rather be there. I miss it," he said. "Sick, isn't it?"

"No," she said. "I imagine you made friends." *And saw some of them die.*

He seemed to be thinking the same thing, because his eyes stared a thousand yards away from her.

"I've never felt that alive," he said.

Outside the mine, near the soft drink machine, the ice dispenser chattered.

Martin jumped, alert.

Suddenly he looked hollow-cheeked, wary, different.

Then, he tried to shrug it off. "How do you like my car?" He gestured to the nearest vehicle, a cactus-colored '69 Mustang, dappled with snow.

Keti said nothing, but met his eyes. *Now, he's lost his innocence,* she thought, and she was profoundly sad for him. She'd grown used to her own cynicism, her own lack of interest in so many things, her single-minded pursuit of survival. But her own feelings made the innocent humanity of others seem more precious, something to be appreciated and guarded.

So she smiled. "I'm glad that you came and found me."

* * *

He followed her to her own house and came inside, waited in her plainly furnished living room, while she went into her bedroom and changed for Christmas Eve at his parents'. When she reappeared, she found him examining a photo of her with her father—Keti on Luther Whitechapel's shoulders at a company picnic.

He turned, stretching his tall body, and scrutinized her outfit. Flared jeans, peasant blouse, long leather coat she'd gotten cheaply at a jumble sale, high platform boots. "Don't suppose you have a couple of pairs of snowshoes around?"

Keti stared. "Why?"

"We could hike to the Old House hot springs."

Keti examined her boots. Another jumble sale purchase, but not for hiking. Though she owned hiking boots, of course. Old ones, from high school. She remembered the Old House hot springs and how, back then, groups of kids would drive over to Bounty to sit in the steaming water, which reeked of sulfur. Sometimes they'd be naked. Sometimes they'd brought beer.

She'd never been part of these excursions.

It occurred to her that Martin was further postponing his return home.

"Dad's snowshoes are around somewhere," she said. "And I have some others that might work. I haven't been on them in *years*." Even as she spoke, she wondered if she should argue with Martin instead, or tell him that it would be okay to go home.

He said, "It's worth checking out. Trying to get to the hot springs."

She thought, selfishly, about how she simply wanted to be alone with him. He was so handsome, with that dark hair sweeping across his forehead, his brown eyes hiding things that she imagined to be deep, meaningful, sensitive, lost—everything ridiculous a teenager might think was there. And *she* was no teenager anymore, and *he* was just like her brother.

Except she'd never been able to make it feel that way.

"Do they know you're coming?"

"Christmas Eve or Christmas Day." He shrugged. "Sometime."

The steam rising from the foul-smelling pool was so thick that Keti could barely make out the shape of the Old House itself. It was a relic of the early mining days and had once been a baron's mansion. Now it was a Victorian ruin. She and Martin had opened the door and peered in, and she'd thought of *Great Expectations,* which she'd read in junior high. She imagined an old lady waiting inside in a yellowed wedding gown.

Then they'd gone to the edge of the pool and stripped off their clothes under the night sky, shielded by the dark and the mist.

Martin was muscular, still beautifully built, and still more handsome because now he was a man. She remembered the gentleness, the inner quiet she used to feel from him. Was it still there? she wondered. Or had war torn it away completely?

Keti watched him across the water, leaning back in the steam, the shades and shapes of his face at peace.

She said, "I'm sorry you had to go through…everything that's happened."

He didn't reply but quickly ducked his head and resurfaced with wet hair, with his straight nose, like an eagle, and the dark eyes that were just hints in the night. His father claimed the Collins family was "Black Irish." Keti had been assured by at least one Irish miner since then that no such group was acknowledged in Ireland. But the Collinses were a handsome family, in a strong and wholesome way. They always seemed to know who they were, and Keti had never seen them in doubt.

Till Martin appeared outside the Empress Mine at the end of her shift.

So clearly unanchored.

What could she say? *What are you going to do, now that you're back?* That would sound like pressure.

He would return to medical school, she assumed. Maybe the army would help him somehow. She was reluctant to press him for details. But Martin would be okay in the long run. After his family surrounded him with their stable, certain love.

She saw his eyes resting on her face, then shifting to her shoulders. Just as he had done, she dunked her head, letting her shoulder-length hair fall back in loose, sleek waves. But not letting her breasts show above the water. Here she was, naked with Martin, as if she did this kind of thing all the time.

But she didn't.

And she'd never before done anything at all like this with him.

He couldn't possibly see her well. But she felt him studying her.

"Darkness is kind," she said, because she didn't want him to forget what she actually looked like in daylight.

He smiled the ghost of a smile. "You think you're not pretty?"

She shrugged, glad he couldn't see her blushing, which she knew she must be. "Not exactly."

"You don't exactly think you're not?"

She tried to think that one through.

"Keti, you've always been pretty. Some people just couldn't see it till you got braces, I guess."

"All people," she corrected.

"You think," he said.

She took the compliment he'd just given her and treasured it, knowing she would think more about it later when she was alone.

But she felt something else in the way he watched her now. It wasn't predatory. But she could tell he was thinking some things through. His voice touched her as he asked, "Are you a virgin?"

"God," she said, and momentarily sank beneath the water again. "No." She didn't look at him.

He came closer to her and pressed his hands against hers under the water, palms together. He didn't try to raise her out of the pool, just laced his fingers with hers. Keti could not breathe, could only feel that his body was separated from hers by a few inches of water—and less. And less. And his forearms, his biceps and triceps, his shoulders, all of him was big and strong, and his hands were *much* bigger than hers.

He said, "I haven't taken things for a test drive since I was hurt. So to speak. Could be a disaster."

She thought, *He'll risk a disaster with me.*

He said, "I don't want a disaster with you."

Her breath caught in her throat. But she couldn't make herself ask what exactly it was that he wanted. Because everything *she* wanted—which was everything, all of him, inside and out—made the stakes much too high.

Martin drew her to him in the water, touching the silkiness of her arms, feeling the strangeness of it all. Keti's touch seemed part of the mineral spring and part of the snow around them and part of the gray of the darkening sky. In the steam, she was an oread, a mountain nymph. He touched her mouth, her firm chin and smooth jaw. He moved closer and kissed her.

Yes, he could want.

Yes, yes, yes.

She kissed him back, and after a moment he said gently, "So you've had lovers?"

She shrugged. "One."

His mouth touched every part of hers, caressing each nerve, one by one.

"It seemed like even when he wanted to please me," she explained, "it was all about what he could *make* me feel. I always thought it could be different then, but I don't really think that anymore."

"Giving up at your age?"

"Don't laugh at me!"

"I'm not."

And their bodies brushed against each other, and she felt her breath grow shallow with the pressure of her breasts against his chest, and more, and more, as he pulled her closer.

"I'm just not *naive* any longer," she said, surprising herself with the bitterness she heard. *And I don't want you to break my heart, because you can, Martin. You are the only person who can!*

He touched her face with hands that seemed to be twice the size of hers. These were a man's hands, rough, strong-fingered working hands. Martin's hands she liked.

His lips caressed hers again, and his hands moved down her body.

This was what frightened her most.

That it was Martin touching her; Martin, the only person she could imagine truly wanting to touch her. It was the crest at the top of a roller coaster, like the roller coaster in Las Vegas she'd once ridden.

They kissed again, and now Martin's mouth traveled over her shoulders and down between her breasts. The water was too hot, and Keti let him ease her up to its edge, let him help her find comfort on the wet rocks. She let him open her legs and kiss the insides of her thighs. And touch her.

She cried out, warm and shuddering and liquid, and his hands were there, clasping hers, giving her something to hold on to.

In the fog, with Edith and Marley

Keti's eyes are filled with tears. Martin was her first true lover. That time was the first she'd really loved, really fallen in love.

The truth is, she'd never been in love with anyone but Martin. Could never imagine loving anyone else. Though she'd tried. Oh, how she'd tried.

And so she and Martin nurtured each other there in the hot springs, and she trusted him, trusted he would never hurt her. She'd given her heart to him long ago.

Now to her guide, she says, "I've seen enough, Edith."

The skinny dog beside her whines, and Keti crouches down to stroke his fur.

"My time grows short!" says Edith. "Quick!"

The Collins house, that same Christmas

"Martin! Martin's home!" exclaimed Amy, all wild, curly long hair and dangling beaded earrings. She whispered to Keti, "You brought him. I didn't think he'd really come."

Keti embraced her friend gladly. Though Bridget was her own age, it was Amy to whom she'd been closer when she lived with the Collinses. Amy with her irreverent sense of humor and her unblushing observations on all aspects of life.

"Oh, Martin! Martin!" said Mrs. Collins.

The entire family was there, from teenage George and Paul to Bridget and newly-married Amy with her husband, Ely, whom she'd met her first year of college.

"Your room is ready for you," Peggy Collins told her son, plucking at Martin's sleeve almost as if she was afraid he'd be taken from her.

"Thanks, Mom."

Keti saw shades of the old Martin then, the Martin who wanted to lighten his mother's load.

They sat around the tree eating Christmas cookies, and Martin opened gifts, going through the motions of acting normal and then, in a quiet moment, clasping Keti's hand.

Amy, in the process of reaching for another cookie, lifted her eyebrows and flashed a look of amusement at Keti. Then, with her parents out of the room, George quietly reading and husband Ely trying to work out a puzzle someone had given him, she focused her gaze on her oldest brother. "So does everything work?"

Her husband dropped his puzzle. "Amy!"

George lowered his book.

Martin moved gently toward his sister and calmly took her forearm, holding it firmly as he began to tickle her.

"No! Help! Mom! Help! George! Someone! My husband, please!" Amy shrieked, hysterical with laughter, thrashing about until he pinned her other arm, as well.

Ely deliberately picked up his puzzle and resumed his study of it.

Through the window, in the fog

Keti gazes at the face of the young Amy, her best woman friend back then.

"She had a large heart!" Edith declares.

Marley sniffs some bushes nearby and lifts his leg against one.

"So she had," whispers Keti.

"She died a woman," Edith says. "And had children."

"One child."

"That's right. Martin's niece, Tiffany."

Keti feels uneasy, remembering the poinsettia on her table, the imperiously-worded yet harmless invitation from Tiffany. "Yes."

What would Amy think, if she knew with what scorn Keti treated her only child—her orphaned child?

Tiffany's an adult, Keti tells herself. *I owe her nothing.*

But she remembers that today, December twenty-fourth, is Tiffany's birthday.

Well, I sent flowers. Her assistant did, anyway. Keti had written a note about it the week before. Now, she sniffs it off, all of it. Flowers are generous, under the circumstances. In any circumstances.

A station wagon outside Bounty

"Please stop, Ely!"

Snow was falling heavily, and Amy was in the back on the folded-down seats, alternately lying on sleeping bags and then kneeling on all fours.

Keti crouched beside her friend and repeated the

plea to Amy's husband to pull over. They were not going to make it to the hospital. Even in the dark, Keti could see something she was pretty damned sure was the baby's head. In all her twenty-five years, she'd never experienced anything that remotely compared to this.

They had been to the hot springs together, the three of them. Amy was overdue, and the warm water had seemed like a good idea. It had done something, all right. When Amy'd stood up, to get out of the hot springs, her waters had broken, splattering and steaming onto the cold rocks, washing over the dusting of snow.

It had been Amy's dream that Martin could be on hand to catch her baby. But he was a resident now, in New Hampshire, and he would be on call over Christmas. So, there he was still in New England, and Amy's baby was almost here and they were *not* at the hospital.

Martin wouldn't be in Bounty for Christmas. The thought that had occurred to Keti so many times over the past weeks, had translated itself into, *Martin is missing the birth of his sister's baby*. But this point also mingled with a resentment entirely of Keti's— not over his finishing medical school, finishing his internship, finishing his residency and becoming the person he was meant to be. It was a resentment that somehow she, Keti Whitechapel, was once again not good enough for Martin Collins.

Their love affair was behind them and yet it seemed to resume whenever he was home. But there was something tentative in all of it. As if Keti were on trial. No, her values were on trial. And she didn't like that at all.

But now Martin was away and Keti was here, and Amy's baby was about to be born right *now*.

I have never seen anything like this. God, you better make this work right, because it's happening, and none of us can stop it.

Ely had obediently pulled over and climbed into the backseat, as well.

Amy pushed out the baby's head in one pop. Keti said, "Oh, God, wait. I think I should check for the cord or something, shouldn't I?"

But she felt no cord around the baby's neck. How did anyone hold on to these slippery things?

Then the baby whooshed into her waiting hands, and her forearms came down to rest on the sleeping bags as she stared in shock and wonder at the strange and perfect infant who had just arrived from another world.

Chapter 6

The fog gives everything a wet kind of coldness. It is an unnatural fog that has Keti clutching Marley's fur, and she thinks that the dog needs a collar and a name tag. I like a dog, she realizes in wonder. I like having a dog, and Marley is my dog.

She recognizes the tree outside the Victorian dwelling. She recognizes the Victorian itself and thinks dimly, *It didn't look so great, did it? I've really made it look nice.*

Because it is *her* house at the time, painted a rather revolting blue with a peeling trim that had originally been burgundy, and as she and Edith approach the porch, Keti recognizes the griffin door knocker.

There is a wreath on the door circling the knocker. Keti herself put up that wreath—a twenty-six-year-old Keti, that is.

A Keti who believed in Christmas, sort of.

A car pulls up to the curb in the fog. It's a Mercedes.

"Marlene!" cries Keti, but the other woman neither hears her nor sees her. Marlene climbs from the car, wrapped in fake fur—fake Dalmatian puppy fur, appallingly—and she seems so young, her face completely unlined. Marlene had always been willing to make time for Keti. The woman who'd once been rejected by her nephew, Keti's father; the woman once considered too immoral to be part of Luther Whitechapel's family circle had always been there for Keti.

But now Keti shivers, remembering her encounter with her great-aunt in the bedroom of this same house, remodeled, perfect, outfitted with every conceivable luxury. Her meeting this Christmas Eve—the meeting that introduced the ghostly Edith. A spectral Marlene in handcuffs.

Keti lets go of that thought, allowing herself the easier comfort of loving the Marlene she remembers.

The Victorian on the Christmas Eve of Tiffany's first birthday
Keti is twenty-six

Keti opened the front door and saw Marlene sweeping up the front steps in her ridiculous Cruella

De Vil coat. Marlene paused dramatically, letting her gaze sweep over the three-story structure, Keti's new home, one of the old miner baron homes of Bounty. "Well, you have your work cut out for you, Keti."

Hurriedly, Keti yanked on a pair of indoor-outdoor mukluks and rushed onto her porch and down to the cracked walkway. She embraced Marlene and arm in arm with her turned to gaze up at the building. "Imagine the *possibilities,* Marlene. I bought this for *half* what I sold Dad's house for."

"Is the roof sound?" Marlene asked doubtfully.

"Barely. I had to do some quick patching for winter, and I'm redoing it properly in the spring. But there are no rodents or spiders or disgusting things— anymore. And I've given you my room. You'll like it."

"Well, where are *you* going to sleep?"

"In one of the others which is more, well, still a work in progress."

Marlene paused, turning in her high white boots to let her eyes sweep the street. Her Mercedes and Keti's old pickup were the only vehicles beyond the low wrought-iron fence. "Is he coming?"

"Yes," said Keti, "but I'm glad you're here first. Let me grab your bags for you."

"No, dear. We'll let your Martin get them."

"*I* can carry the bags," Keti said. "I don't want him waiting on me…"

"On me. Leave it, Keti," Marlene ordered.

Keti shivered in her thin, red wool sweater. She should have put on a parka before coming outside. "Well, come on in," she relented. "Look, Marlene, here's the thing. Can we not talk about the brothel while Martin's here?"

"Of course, we won't," Marlene agreed. "It's a business matter."

"What I mean is, can we not talk about the fact that I've bought half of the Palomino Palace," Keti clarified.

Her great-aunt gave her a sharp glance. "You're not going to tell him?"

"I am. At the right time. But that might not be tonight. I mean, I don't think any of the Collinses is going to be wild about the idea, and I need to think of exactly what I'm going to say."

Marlene gave an understanding shrug. Following her niece up the porch steps, she said, "Well, if you ever figure out the *right* thing, please tell me. Because for some people… Well, I've never found words that satisfy them. So I've stopped trying. The only time it has ever really mattered," she added as Keti opened the front door, "was when it made a difference as to whether or not you would let me help you after your dad died."

Keti paused in the doorway to hug her only living relative. "It never made any difference at all."

Later that same Christmas

Martin gazes up at the cracked ceiling above the brass bed that Keti had bought at a yard sale. The bed frame is used; the mattress, new. There is another new mattress on the four-poster Marlene is sleeping in. That bed was a Whitechapel family heirloom—which means it was Keti's mother's, actually. She brought it to Bounty with her when she was married.

Keti had been to the Collins house that evening, with Marlene, to celebrate Tiffany's first birthday and also Christmas Eve; Martin had driven them there and then brought them back home.

Martin, the physician.

He would be in Bounty only for a short time, and Keti considered simply not mentioning the brothel. She could let Amy—or more likely, Bridget—write to tell him about it. Because he wasn't exactly planning on hanging around.

No, he was going to India. To work.

"You could come with me," he told Keti now.

"To Calcutta?" She tried to conceal her dismay. Why would he think she'd be remotely tempted by that suggestion?

"You could get nurses' training there. We could be together."

Keti was touched. But she was touched that Martin thought her the kind of person who would become a nurse in an Indian slum? No. She was touched simply by the fact that he wanted her with him. She hadn't expected that. And she had no idea what to do about it. She *did* want to be with Martin. But at the price of living and working in slums, possibly among lepers? *No.* That wasn't for Keti. It would be one thing, maybe, if they could actually make money there. But Martin was volunteering— or something like that. He wouldn't come home with anything more than he'd had when he left—if, that was, he avoided catching whatever terrible diseases they had over there, which Keti doubted he'd manage to do.

So why tell him about the brothels, at all? After all, it would be some time before even Amy or Bridget found out, as long as Keti avoided shouting the news from the rooftops.

Finally, she said to Martin, "I don't think I'm cut out to be a nurse." The problem with *not* telling him about the brothels was that Keti loathed deception and she especially loathed deceiving anyone about who she was. Because if you pretended to be something other than the person you really were and people loved you, they wouldn't actually be loving *you*—they'd be loving someone else.

In any case, though Martin lay on top of her patchwork bedspread with her now, he wasn't making any romantic moves. He'd come upstairs to see the rest of the house, after Marlene had turned in for the night. And now here he was on Keti's "spare room" bed. The spare room being the only bedroom besides her own that was fit to sleep in.

"You think you're cut out for running a mine office? Or whatever it is, exactly, that you do? Speculate in real estate? Buy and sell stocks?"

Keti did a little bit of all of it. She'd bought stock in the ski area, for one thing, and that had worked out exceptionally well. In fact, she now owned almost forty percent of the resort business. And her holdings in the Empress Mine had also done well for her— plus, there was the sale of her father's house. The brothel in which she'd bought a stake was just another way to increase her income, so that she could buy more of the ski area and also invest in another ski area over by Lake Tahoe. The downhill skiing industry was really going to take off soon, and Keti was getting in just in time. She only wished she'd had the toehold she had now ten years ago.

Marlene assured her that Nevada's legal brothels could make her the kind of fast money she needed to increase her real-estate holdings. And so Keti had decided to buy an interest in one of Marlene's operations.

"I think," Keti told Martin, "that I'm cut out to make money. Anyhow, maybe I better, so you have someone to support you when you come back from India." She was half joking and half serious. Was he *ever* going to get interested in actually making a living? Or did he plan to live out his entire life as Saint Francis of Assisi?

Martin laughed, taking no offense at her remark.

But Keti had a feeling close to certainty that he would take offense when he learned about the brothel.

She wavered again. *He doesn't need to learn about it from me. It's none of his business, anyhow.*

"No, seriously," Martin said. "Don't you want to…contribute something to the world?"

Keti searched her heart. Contribute something? She had no calling to be a doctor, for instance, as Martin had.

No, Martin would not understand about the brothel. Martin simply didn't think money was important. As for contributing something to the world…

"Not especially," she said.

And she felt him look at her differently after that, felt him see her as someone who didn't care about others.

Well, let him. It was better for him to see her as she was.

Outside her home, with Edith

"All right, he wasn't happy about the brothels," Keti admits. After all, there was more than one, after her first venture into the business succeeded so well.

She didn't want to see any more of these Christmases with Edith. What was the point?

But already they were outside Bounty, away from the trees, beneath a neon sign that jutted out against the wide Nevada sky.

The Christmas Eve of Tiffany's second birthday

The brothel lights were a small part of Palomino Palace's Christmas decorations.

"Yo, ho, my girls!" said Marlene, stepping back inside: "No more work tonight. Christmas Eve, Carlene! Christmas Eve, my sweet Keti! Christmas Eve…"

Keti had turned twenty-seven this year, and she'd decided not to go to the Collins house for Christmas Eve despite Mrs. Collins's and Amy's repeated invitations. *It won't be Christmas without you, Keti!*

And it was Tiffany's birthday.

And she, Keti, was Tiffany's godmother.

Well, she would like to oblige Amy in this, in spending Tiffany's second birthday with the Collins family, but the price was too steep. She simply wasn't going.

Not after the things Martin had said and done the last time they'd talked, when he'd returned from India in October to set up a practice back home.

The bastard.

St. Martin, M.D.

Now, at the Palomino Palace, somebody plugged in the jukebox and people began to dance.

The phone rang, the private office line, not the main business phone. Keti got up, walking toward the office in her tight purple stonewashed jeans, on her pink patent leather heels. Christmas clothes. Fun clothes.

She spent little time there. Now she owned it outright and paid Marlene to run it, which her great-aunt did as well as managing her own brothels. *Keti, it's a good business, but you don't want to be involved in the running of it.*

Keti couldn't have, if she'd wanted to. She didn't have that kind of time, now that she was so busy managing her other investments, especially the mine company, and serving on the board of directors for the corporation that owned the Bounty ski resort and its sister area near Lake Tahoe.

Passing two of the girls—two of the prostitutes—in flannel pajamas and fluffy slippers, carrying packages, Keti reached the office and picked up the phone. "Hello?"

"Keti."

She tensed. Why on earth was he even bothering to call? She didn't want to hear anything he had to say to her, unless what he had to say had changed, which she doubted. "Hello, Martin."

A silence that wasn't entirely silent, because she could hear, faintly, all the usual happy sounds of the Collins house at Christmas.

She had loved Martin dearly, but she didn't love him now. She couldn't love anyone who sat in judgment of her for being who she was.

Martin had refused to give Bounty's brothel prostitutes the health checks that were required by the state of Nevada, leaving it to his partner to handle that part of the practice. Which saved both of them from nasty lawsuits. Because Martin never *said* that he wouldn't do the health checks. It was simply the case that his partner did them all.

"It doesn't seem the same here without you," he said.

"Thank you." Her voice was toneless. She wasn't spending much time in Bounty these days, anyhow. Her most time-consuming work was across the state, in the corporate offices of Ameri-Metals in Elko. She could have worked from Bounty, but Martin's silent—and articulated—disapproval had eroded all the love from their relationship, leaving only a *need* within her to be free and do what she wanted to do. Which was the entire point. If you had enough money, no one could hurt you.

Martin disagreed. Martin helped the poor families of Bounty, willingly serving all those who had been affected by the Empress Mine's closing. And acting as if the mine's closing, which Keti hoped would be brief, was *her* fault.

People had to go where the work was and where the money was, and it was that simple. It was what she'd done. In Elko, an AmeriMetals silver mine continued to flourish.

"What are you doing?" he asked.

He knew where she was—he'd called the brothel, after all. How he'd known where to find her, she couldn't guess. Still, he would have known that she would spend Christmas with Marlene.

"Oh, Marlene closes for Christmas Eve and Christmas—well, till six tomorrow evening."

"*You* close," he replied.

"Well, yes. It's Marlene's decision, but it's fine. Though we could stay open. Men keep leaning on the bell outside. And the girls here would work. They like to make money." *They choose this life, Martin. Nobody makes them. Don't you get it?*

"Like you."

"Alas. The great crime. Capitalism."

"That's not what I mean."

"You don't need to elaborate," she told him, vividly remembering the last time he had done so.

"You fear the world too much, Keti."

"I'm not listening to this, Martin. I do *not* fear anything."

"Other people, maybe?" he said.

"If I'm not afraid of *you*," she said, "who else would I be afraid of?"

He laughed. Tenderly.

Unexpectedly, her eyes watered.

"All your other hopes have merged into the single hope of being absolutely 'secure,'" he said. "I've seen your nobler aspirations fall away one by one, as you've come to focus entirely on Gain. Haven't I?"

"What nobler aspirations?" she asked, with a brittle smile he couldn't see. "I was never like you, Martin. I was never good."

"I thought you were. You used to lie yourself blue in the face to keep the rest of us out of trouble. When we were young kids, and when we were teenagers. Sometimes you let yourself get into trouble so that no one else would be punished. And you used to like knitting things for people. When you lived with my family, remember you knit secret presents for some of the kids in town."

"It was a church project! I had to do it. Don't credit me with your own generosity, Martin. It's just not me, all right?"

"Wrong. You are changed. You're a different woman."

"And before I was a girl. Whom you never looked at, because of at least one thing I didn't have that money could buy." She was thinking of braces, straight teeth. Not to mention fashionable clothes. But straight teeth on their own would have made such a difference back then. "Remember?"

"I remember that we were happy when we were one in heart."

Keti considered hanging up the phone. "We never have been."

"Come home. Free yourself from that world. Keti, you bought a *brothel*. Those women are prisoners."

"These women," she replied coldly, "would be insulted to hear you say that. They make good money, and that's why they're here."

"And you make good money, too, from what they do."

Silence.

She wondered if he was reflecting on his own generosity and benevolence.

They'd had this conversation before. Even before Martin had gone to work in India, they'd seemed to be drifting further and further apart. Yet the attraction remained.

Until this summer.

No, I'm not attracted to you any more, he'd said. *How could I be, knowing the kind of person you've become?*

He'd made her cry, and afterward he'd apologized, but the apology had been meaningless.

Keti wasn't sure anything had ever hurt so much.

And she'd decided she didn't like *him.*

"This doesn't affect you," she said now. "It has nothing to do with you. It's not like I'm your wife or even your girlfriend. In fact, I'm not a family member at all. It would be different if you were actually part of my life."

He said, "I can't live with money made that way, Keti."

That was *it.* "Nobody has invited you to," she said firmly. She set the receiver back in the cradle and calmly gave it the finger.

Carlene, one of the girls, paused in the doorway, grinning slightly. "Who pissed *you* off?"

A foggy night, on a snow-covered mountain road

"I'm stuck with you right now, aren't I?" Keti asks. "I can't escape what you intend to show me."

"What is it that you don't want to see?" Edith asks.

Keti considers the question. She thinks most of all about Martin. She has made it a practice *not* to remember—not to dwell on the past. *I can't have Martin. That's why I stopped thinking about it.*

She hadn't continued to hate Martin as she'd hated him that one Christmas. He'd apologized, and he'd really meant it, and he'd told Keti that he loved her.

Still, she doesn't answer the ghost of Edith, the ghost who is about to unfold another Christmas Past.

Two years on, Christmas Eve

Keti's Mercedes convertible was not made for the snow, and there was plenty of that in Bounty this year. So she'd left it in Elko and rented this Jeep. Aunt Marlene would be joining her at the Collins home the following morning. But tonight Marlene was visiting her brothels and distributing gifts to her girls.

Keti was working and living in Elko now, though she still owned her home in Bounty. She wouldn't have agreed to return to Bounty for Christmas if it hadn't been for Amy and her husband's deaths in a car crash—which had left poor Tiffany an orphan, to be raised by Bridget.

And Bridget, even for Keti, could never replace Amy.

She and Martin had simply called a halt to all discussion of her brothels, her mines and what he referred to as her "pursuit of Gain." Maybe, Keti thought, the realities of maintaining his own medical practice had begun to sink in. He had to pay for little necessities like malpractice insurance, after all.

But the population of Bounty was still inclined to canonize him.

Well, that was fine. What he did with his life didn't affect her.

She'd promised to meet him at his house, an old

Victorian "shotgun," long and narrow, and ride with him to his parents' home.

His Nissan truck was parked outside, coated with fresh snow. Keti sighed when she saw it.

If only Martin were different—or if she were different. She still had precious recollections of those few months they'd shared right after he'd returned from Vietnam, when the two of them had been everything to each other. But then he'd gone back to medical school, and his vocation had become both his wife and his mistress, and their relationship had headed downhill from there.

Too much trying to change each other.

Too much of Martin trying to change me, that is.

In recent years, there had been a couple of other men in Keti's life. Two, to be exact. Neither had offered even a single enjoyable experience. Neither had succeeded in making her forget Martin. The lovemaking that she'd known with him was still the only real *lovemaking* of her entire life. Yes, other men had been with her. But she'd never *enjoyed* it. Not once.

What she still longed for, sometimes, was to be with Martin again as they used to be.

But that would require her to play by his rules. And clearly she was *not* a saint and *not* a do-gooder. Early on, she'd been on the receiving end of plenty of that sort of energy, and it had driven her to stand on her own feet.

Parking at the curb in front of his house, she

climbed out of the rented Jeep. It wasn't much of a house. He could do better, Keti knew, if only he would save some of his money instead of giving it away to all and sundry, including his parents and Bridget. Granted, there was nothing wrong with the upkeep on the house. The pale yellow siding and white trim had both recently been painted. And his mother had sewn the curtains that hung in the few windows.

A cat leaped to the porch as Keti approached. It was a grey tabby with three legs. *Honestly, Martin. Can't you even get yourself a decent pet?*

Martin opened the door before she reached the first step.

At thirty-two, he was even more attractive than he'd been as a boy. His features, rough, angular, seemed so much better suited to a grown man. He wore canvas pants and a dark red pile sweater with navy trim on the cuffs, collar and pocket. He said, "Hi," and embraced her briefly and casually.

The distance between them yawned like a chasm, and Keti yearned for things to be as they'd once been. *They can't be. I'm too different. And he doesn't like who I really am.*

While all the time, she continued to love and admire him. Which was, she thought, pathetic.

Keti now wore her blond hair shoulder-length. The curls bounced against the collar of her sheepskin jacket. She was dressed in suede pants and boots. She'd done everything she could with her appearance, yet Martin didn't seem to notice.

It was freezing outside. She hoped his heater worked. "Let's go in my truck," he said. "You can leave your vehicle here."

This seemed positive to Keti. There'd been no clear discussion about where she should sleep. She said, "Are you spending the night there?"

"I thought I would. My parents like it on Christmas Eve. And they're planning to have you stay with them, as well."

Keti knew.

She'd agreed to sleep over, like one of the family, instead of returning to her own house, the Victorian whose restoration was the closest thing she had to a hobby.

If she left the Jeep at Martin's, she couldn't duck out of the celebration at the Collins house if things became uncomfortable there. Of course, the thing most likely to make things uncomfortable was Martin himself. But hadn't she agreed to stay with his parents especially because she wanted to see him?

Hopeful, always hopeful, like a puppy. No wonder she didn't like dogs. Or cats, either.

"I'll ride with you," she said.

Martin helped load her luggage and her bags of gifts into his pickup. He carried out his own bag, which had been sitting by the front door, as well. He did not invite her to have a look around his house, but said only, "You need to use the bathroom or anything?"

"No. I'm fine." *You break my heart with every word you say, Martin Collins, you self-righteous jerk.*

"How's your practice?" she asked, ignoring the fact that he still refused to perform health exams on the girls from her brothels. She chose to pretend that despite this decision he still respected her. But in her heart, she knew he didn't.

"Can't complain. Actually, I love it. I feel close to everyone in town."

He'd just been named Bounty's citizen of the year.

"Still getting along with your partner?" she asked. The physician he shared his practice with was ten years older than Martin.

"Yes, but actually he's moving and I haven't found a replacement yet."

"In that case, I assume you'll be prepared to take care of the health checks for my girls," she said.

He opened the passenger door of the truck for Keti, then got in on his side and looked at her. "How can you be okay with it, Keti? How would you like to be one of them?"

It was an argument they'd had many times before, and now Keti really felt like fighting. "I could have been. But I never chose to be. They've chosen it. What's more, they're safe. In my brothels, they have physical protection and their health is safeguarded, too. Prostitution has always existed and it always will."

"Sure. But how can you make money from it, Keti? How would you like handing over fifty percent of your earnings to a female pimp?"

She fastened her seat belt. "If my fifty percent was what those girls are making, I wouldn't mind in the least." She considered. "Though, being me, I'm sure I'd try to find a way to keep it all."

"But surely you wouldn't turn tricks," he said.

"I don't know. Maybe I would have," she replied, not certain it was the truth but saying the words anyhow. "Of course, now I make better money doing what I do."

He started the engine. "You could do something good with your life, Keti."

He was, she told herself, such a judgmental pain. She only loved him as a brother. And she changed the subject. "How are your folks doing?"

She asked because of Amy and Ely's deaths.

With all her business travel, she hadn't seen much of the Collins family this year. And given these kinds of scenes with Martin, it had been more comfortable that way.

"Somehow, they take everything in stride. But it made them older, for sure. They *look* older. They've focused on Tiffany, though, on making sure she has everything they can possibly give her." He pulled away from the curb.

"How is she?"

"I'm not sure. Bridget is such a different kind of mom from how Amy was."

Keti didn't need that explained. Bridget had always been more uptight than her older sister. "You must miss her," she told Martin. "Amy, I mean." *I do,* she thought. Martin might judge her, but Amy never had.

"Yes." The roads were white with fresh snow, and Martin drove slowly. "You were there when Tiffany was born, Keti. You caught her as she came into the world. You took care of Amy and her baby. That was noble." He bit back whatever else he might have said.

Keti remembered the Christmas Eve Tiffany was born in the back of that station wagon. It was, she thought, the best thing she'd ever done.

But now Amy was gone, and she could hardly stand to remember it.

"Well," she said, "it's not the kind of thing I could do for a living."

"Why not?" he asked.

"Be serious. I'd have to go to medical school, and I'm not smart enough. *And* I'm already twenty-nine. I'm too old."

"You're definitely not too old. Anyhow, I wasn't suggesting that you become a physician. You could be a maternity nurse. Hell, you could work in my practice. Or you could become a midwife, though that takes a little more training."

"None of those jobs pay well enough," she replied bluntly.

"Why do you need more money?"

"Because *that's* what I'm good at," she said. "It's the most important thing in the world to me. I write down my financial goals every year, and I achieve them."

Martin drove slowly down the street and turned onto the evergreen-lined avenue leading to his parents' house. "But you don't do anything with the money, Keti. I mean, you have nice clothes and a nice car and some nice property. But all those things are just...things."

"Just things?" She squinted at him and shook her head. "They matter to me. And I give my ten percent to charities, just the way a good Christian is supposed to."

She saw, again, a pursing of his lips that told her he was biting his tongue.

"Just say it," she snapped.

"Jesus didn't put the figure at ten percent."

"You are so holier-than-thou I'm sometimes astonished you're still walking among us, Martin Collins. Any day, I expect you to be officially recognized as a saint."

He blushed. His cheeks were freshly shaven and Keti plainly saw his color change.

Then he laughed softly. "I think I need you around, Keti, to keep me in my place."

Her heart warmed, and she almost dared to hope again. It was foolish to be a grown woman capable of loving only this one difficult man. Martin hadn't invited her to spend Christmas with him so that they could renew their old romance. But, yes, she *had* come with the hope of, well, renewing what had been.

And what if she was as he wanted her to be? She could *imagine* herself a nurse in his practice. But she couldn't imagine *not* being at the helm of her own businesses.

She wished she was a better woman, but she felt miserably that she never could be. She would so much rather have money and things and *certainty*— much rather that than do and think the kinds of things that would make a positive difference in the world.

And when it came down to it, she always faced the fact that if he couldn't love her as she was—well, he couldn't really love her.

Keti had never seen Mrs. Collins cry, and this Christmas was no different. "I am so thankful," she said repeatedly, "for the four children and three grandchildren I have." Bridget and her husband had two children, in addition to the orphaned Tiffany, who was four years old tonight. "I'm also thankful for *you,* Keti. My bonus daughter."

Keti was touched. And she believed that Mrs. Collins actually felt what she said, actually believed it; she was *grateful* for her lot in life. It was no wonder, Keti thought, that Martin had turned into such a good person when he'd been raised by such a woman.

The whole family walked to midnight mass, Martin carrying Tiffany, who was sound asleep in her red velvet dress, white tights and navy coat.

Keti couldn't help smiling as Bridget's two daughters whispered in the row behind Keti and Martin and snickered over the priest's unusually high voice. Bridget cast them a furious look, but that did nothing to settle them down.

Impulsively, as she sang, *"Silent night, holy night..."* Keti touched Martin's arm. Little Tiffany lay asleep on the pew between him and his mother.

He took Keti's hand, and his fingers interlaced with hers and squeezed, and he did not release her.

"Holy infant, so tender and mild..."

His baritone was strong and tuneful beside her alto. At the kiss of peace, Martin embraced her and looked into her blue eyes with his warm brown ones. "Merry Christmas, Keti."

Oh, God, she thought. *If I could only stop loving him.*

* * *

Bridget's girls and Tiffany went to sleep in Bridget's old room. Keti would sleep in the room that she and Amy had once shared, directly across the hall from Martin's on the second floor.

She was dressed for bed in soft blue flannel pajamas decorated with white snowflakes when there came a knock at her door. Expecting Mrs. Collins with a last offer of extra blankets, Keti went to the door and opened it.

Martin stood there with a small box wrapped in red paper and adorned with a gold ribbon. He held it out to her.

Keti gave a dry laugh. "I thought you didn't get me anything."

"I have *never* given you nothing for Christmas."

"Actually, you have." That first year they were lovers. But then he'd given her something so much better than a gift—himself. Now she would gladly trade whatever was in the package for some affection, for the smallest sign that he still loved her.

Well, maybe the gift was that sign.

She thought of her present to him, a recent novel, beneath the tree downstairs. Hardly intimate. Deliberately sibling-like, that gift was. She'd wanted it to be so.

Now she unwrapped the box and lifted the lid. She

had to fold back red-and-gold tissue paper to see what lay within. A watch.

It was exquisite, Black Hills Gold in three colors. The cuff-style band was decorated with a design of hearts and leaves. The face was black, with gold filigree hands.

"Look inside," Martin said.

She turned it and read the inscription on the smooth interior of the band: Bah! Humbug.

Keti tried not to frown, tried not to show the hurt she felt. There was teasing, and then there was *mean* teasing. Nonetheless, she understood. Martin still hoped for some change in her. "I'm not a Scrooge, Martin."

"It was affectionately meant." Then, he swore and pulled her into his arms. "Keti, I didn't mean to hurt you. I wouldn't hurt you for anything."

"You hurt me all the time!" she exclaimed, unable to keep from saying so. "You always want me to be some other person, someone I'm not, some imagined person *you* create. And I'm so far from that it's not even worth my trying to be better, by your rules."

"I love you as you are," he said fiercely, and she saw his eyes were on hers. "That's what that watch means, Keti. I'm not laughing at you. I'm doing what you said, loving *you*."

"Scrooge."

His hands tipped back her head as he kissed her face. "I know why you do it, Keti."

"Why I do what?"

"Why you live the way you do."

"I don't want to talk about this," she said, struggling for self-control.

"We don't have to. I'm just saying that I understand why you feel as you do about money. You're scared. You've *been* poor, and you never want to be poor again. But the only true wealth in this world, Keti, is the people around you."

"Will you stop? Just for five seconds, please stop trying to change me, and stop preaching. It's not your most attractive habit."

She saw him grapple with the fact that he had been preaching, as she'd said. He stopped, bent his head to hers and their lips touched.

They moved to the single bed, and Martin wrapped himself around her. Keti was safe, then. This was the only safe place. It seemed to her, for an instant, that if she could just be the woman he wanted her to be, she would always be safe.

The only trouble was, she wouldn't be herself.

And now Keti was torn between the joy she felt in his arms and the sense that his love for her now was in no way linked to commitment. This was a love that acknowledged their differences and their different paths, a love that imposed a casualness on even this meeting.

And yet their mouths together produced the same desire.

Martin had a condom.

"I'm appalled," she said, "that you're prepared."

"You're the only one I make love with," he said flatly. "Why *wouldn't* I be ready?"

The words soothed her troubled spirit. *You're the only one I make love with.*

Martin felt comfort in his own torn spirit once more as he entered her body, trying to understand her, hungry to be inside her every cell, to know her utterly. Wanting to be enough for Keti.

Enough.

That was always the thing with her. What was *enough?*

No love *could* ever be sufficient. Over the years he'd known her as an adult, he'd learned to face that fact. Keti loved money, and to her it was like air— an absolute essential. Not an ordinary amount of money, but an amount she believed would make her completely invulnerable.

And this financial success was having its effect, he knew, because he could see the signs that she had grown calloused.

The brothels.

With the starlight and moonlight and Christmas

lights outside the window, Martin could see Keti's pale hair, her smooth features. She was lovely.

He touched her lips and felt her writhe beneath him, trying to draw even closer, and the shudders of her orgasms, those multiple orgasms that seemed to go on forever, that brought him deeper into her, trying not to cry out himself. Letting go.

"Why can't this be enough, Keti?"

Keti's head snapped up. "Why can't it be enough for *you?* I don't notice you trying to see me more often, even as a friend. I don't notice you asking me to marry you. Because *I'm* not enough."

"That's not true."

She waited for an explanation, an elaboration.

None was offered.

Martin saw that she wasn't going to change, even though his definition of love was that two people who loved each other would make each other better.

The way for Martin to become better, if he were to be with Keti, was to learn to tolerate the differences between them.

He didn't know why it was so hard for him.

Or why he was so attracted to a woman whose values were so repellent.

She said softly, "I don't see what it matters to you

anyway. You don't... Well, you don't want to be with me in any permanent way."

It was the second time tonight she'd said that. "I would, Keti."

She seemed to hesitate—over what, he didn't know. "Would, if what? If I was different?"

"I..." Words caught in his throat. "I can't visualize it, with you as you are. But I *want* it."

And he felt how tightly she clung to him, as if she were drowning and only he could keep her head above water.

Through that cloudy water, he imagined a disturbing illusion and he wondered if it was becoming real. Could it be that Keti was as she was and becoming more that way, greedier, more selfish, because he was as he was?

No. I make my choices. She makes hers. One doesn't create the other.

But if all people were connected, couldn't it be true that his withholding love and commitment from her worked as a catalyst and made her less loving, in turn?

Christmas Day, the same year

"Keti!" Aunt Marlene took her great-niece in her arms and kissed her. "How beautiful you look."

"You, too," Keti said truthfully. *May I age that well,* she thought.

But fresh from Martin's arms, now only hours away from the memory of his touch, she was also thinking that Marlene looked harder than she, Keti, remembered.

"And Martin," Marlene said, embracing him next. "Bounty's physician looks so well."

"Thank you." His smile was quiet but unreserved.

The Collinses were gushing over Marlene, and Peggy took her white fur coat to hang up, exclaiming, "Isn't this beautiful?"

Marlene had brought gifts for everyone. For Bridget's daughters and for Tiffany there were Barbie dolls and a Barbie Dream House and a pink Corvette. For Martin's brothers, ski sweaters from Norway— and the same for Martin and his father. And so on. Much more expensive gifts than Keti had brought, but Keti wasn't comfortable making such a big splash. It was simply unnecessary. She and Marlene sat together on the couch in the living room, admiring the Christmas tree and catching up on each other's lives. When the others in the room were busy playing a game of Skittles, Marlene quietly asked Keti, "And what about Martin?"

"What about him?" Keti replied, just as quietly.

"Are you two still feuding?"

"We *don't* feud. He just wants me to be different from how I am. From who I am," she added, almost to herself.

"It's dangerous," Marlene told her, "to change yourself for a man."

"Don't you think I know that?" Keti hadn't meant to snap. "Anyhow, I couldn't if I wanted to. So that's that."

And then she showed Marlene the watch that Martin had given her the night before.

When she read the inscription inside, Marlene laughed, then squeezed her great-niece's hand. "Don't worry, Keti. I love you. And so, I suspect, does he."

So he says, Keti thought, smiling ruefully as she clasped the watch back on her wrist.

Chapter 7

"No more," Keti begs the ghost of her child-hood playmate Edith.

"Is something troubling you, Keti?" Edith asks.

"What is the use in looking back?"

"To see where your life has taken you. In order to make use of the time you still have."

The time she still has. Keti looks at her wrist. The gold watch is not there just now. It's at home in the top drawer of her nightstand. She still wears it, yes.

Bah! Humbug.

No, that isn't how she feels about Christmas at all. Not now.

She and Edith and Marley stop outside another

house in Bounty, and Keti regards the relatively
sedate neon sign outside. The Last Resort—Girls,
Girls, Girls.

Ah. Her other brothel.

Two more Christmases must have passed. Two?·
Yes. She was thirty-one that year; Keti remembers it
well.

She'd been living back at home and had begun to
work exclusively from Bounty, traveling as seldom
as possible, trying to be part of Martin's life.

The result was another rift, of course.

And this particularly snowy night.

Fatima was six feet tall, with the exquisitely
sculpted cheekbones of a native of Somalia. How she
had ended up working as a brothel prostitute in
Bounty, Nevada, was a long story, involving her sister
Sammar, a wealthy man and Sammar's determination that Fatima not be subjected to what she,
Sammar, had been through. Ritual female circumcision, which compared in no way, Keti now understood, to male circumcision as it was practiced in the
western world.

Keti discovered this only because Sammar was in
the brothel tonight, Christmas Eve. Well, it was
Christmas Day, in fact 2:00 a.m. And Sammar, who
was pregnant but was being allowed to visit Fatima
for the holidays, was in labor.

"You have to go to the hospital," Keti said.

"No. No hospital."

Fatima, whose English was much better than her older sister's, explained that at the hospital the baby would be delivered by cesarian section, which was against Sammar's beliefs—except to save the mother's life, that is.

Keti was damned sure that prostitution—legal brothel prostitution, as Fatima practiced it, and also hooking in Las Vegas, as Sammar did—was also against their religious beliefs. The sisters' situations troubled her in a way such things usually didn't. Sammar had believed she could become a model in the United States. Both she and her little sister had been taken to Las Vegas, and modeling had never been part of the picture. Now, Fatima, at least, was better off. She lived at the Last Resort for three weeks of every month and in a trailer in Bounty, which she now owned, for the remainder of the time. No pimp.

So why did it bother Keti so much?

Probably because it was so clear to her that neither of these women had initially planned to become a whore. Now one of them—who was no responsibility of Keti's whatsoever—was in labor in Keti's brothel. "Well, maybe it will save her life," Keti reasoned with Fatima.

"She knows she can have her baby the regular way, as she would at home."

How Sammar's pimp had allowed the pregnancy to happen mystified Keti as much as anything else. She herself felt no joy or excitement over the situation. It was all ghastly. The identity of the baby's father was unknown to Sammar. Her pimp might even be the father.

I can't take care of this woman or her baby.

But Sammar was crying and Fatima was holding her hand, and her eyes pleaded with Keti.

Fatima was the highest earner in either of Keti's brothels.

Keti did need to take care of Fatima, which meant helping Fatima to believe that her life at the Last Resort was a good one. So she said she would take a look at Sammar's labor, which seemed quite advanced. Why hadn't Fatima come to her earlier in the evening? But maybe she, like her sister, had been afraid that Keti would force Sammar to go to the hospital.

It was when Keti agreed to look at Sammar that she discovered why western physicians would choose to deliver Sammar's baby by cesarean section—and why Sammar had wanted to spare her younger sister the painful ritual she had experienced as a child.

The woman had no vulva that Keti could see. It was baffling to Keti that Sammar managed to work as a prostitute at all, and still harder to imagine that she'd ever become pregnant, given what had been done to her. Yes, there was an opening, but there was certainly no sign of elasticity. The last thing Keti wanted to do was hurt the feelings of Fatima's sister; after all, this was the way the woman was. What could she do about it?

She belongs in the hospital, she thought.

"Will you please let me get you to a doctor?" she asked.

Tears and hysterical head-shaking from Sammar.

If this woman died here at the brothel, there would be no end to the trouble and red tape. Keti might somehow even be accused of manslaughter.

The answer seemed obvious. Call 911, have Sammar transported to the hospital and pay the medical bills, as a gift to Fatima.

It wasn't what she did.

Instead, Keti hurried out of Fatima's suite and down the hall to the office. She knew Martin's home number. She never used it, but she knew it. *He'll be at the Collins house, though.*

"Hello?"

"Thank God. Martin, it's Keti. Please come over. There's a pregnant woman here, not one of mine, but a sister. She had something done to her in Africa, and it doesn't look, well, *usual* to me."

"Tell me."

"She's in labor, Martin. Can't you just come?"

"Why don't you take her to the emergency room?"

Tersely, she explained.

"This kind of thing could cost me my license, Keti."

"Well, it's not the world's best situation for me, either. But, I'm telling you, it's demeaning to this woman to have her baby by cesarean, and her life's bad enough as it is. She's determined to give birth vaginally. And actually, I believe she can. Damn it, Martin, can't you please just *help?*"

Silence. Then, "I'll stop by."

"I don't think we have a lot of time. She's not in a good way."

"Is the baby crowning?"

"God, what do I know? Everything looks different, but I think I can see the baby's head. Please *come.*"

It was clear to Martin that now there was no time for the hospital, barely time for a local anesthetic to take effect before he performed an episiotomy to make it possible for Sammar to push the baby out. In Somalia, did the women simply tear? he wondered. He handled only the most routine pregnancies in his own practice, referring complicated cases to obstetricians in the nearest larger city.

Keti assisted him in Fatima's rooms at the brothel, and two of the other women came in to watch, as well, though Keti sent one outside with a flea in her ear for making noises of disgust and horror at Sammar's mutilated genitals. Martin silently applauded her action. He wouldn't have thought of it, but Keti was right to make Sammar feel she was beautiful rather than an object of disgust just because she looked different from Western women.

Keti and Fatima supported Sammar, holding her up as she squatted, helping her move to a hands-and-knees posture when she was ready to do that.

The baby came out in two pushes, certainly not the most elegant birth Martin had ever attended.

Afterward, they eased Sammar back against the pillows on the bed, and Keti said, "Here's your little girl," handing her the infant, wrapped in a warm bath towel.

Sammar looked at the newborn with oddly expressionless eyes.

The eyes, Keti realized, of a prostitute.

A streetwalker, she told herself.

Because Fatima wasn't like that.

Not yet, Keti.

A later Christmas, a few years on

Fog swirled outside Keti's restored Bonanza Victorian. A Christmas party was in progress, and the curb outside was lined with Mercedes-Benz sedans, even a Jaguar, so ill-suited to a Nevada winter. But there was that old pickup truck of Martin's, too.

"Hey, Bobby, check this out." One of the unruly sons of Martin's brother Paul held up a piece of

Keti's Spode china. He made as if to drop it, saying, "Oops," and both boys laughed.

Keti noticed them as she came down the stairs, stepped into the dining room and relieved them of the plate. "Thank you," she said matter-of-factly. She was an attractive woman at thirty-five, though her appearance had become the slightest bit brittle. Her blond hair was carefully styled now in order to look *unstyled.* It fell to her shoulders in loose curls that were casual and soft and succeeded in looking expensive. She wore a black sequined dress, long-sleeved and backless, with black patent leather pumps.

She put away the plate and glanced into the dining room. There, Martin's niece, Tiffany, was picking her way through a piece on the baby grand piano while Bridget sat beside her. Martin stood near the French doors talking to his father.

Keti's heart was broken. No, not broken. It wasn't that. But somewhere in the past few years she'd lost Martin's love. When he saw her now, he never had the old affection in his eyes. Instead, he kept her at a careful distance. He was uninterested in her and he took pains to make it obvious. Not that she feared there was another woman in his life. In Bounty, she would have known if that were the case. There were no secrets in a town this size.

She'd sold the brothels, sold them in the year after the birth of Sammar's daughter. She'd sold them to

Marlene, telling her aunt a lie Marlene hadn't believed. But Marlene hadn't pressed her. Keti had told Martin that it was none of his business why.

The truth? Simply, that time there had been something about the way Sammar had looked when Keti had handed her that baby…

Well, it reminded me of me.

Which made no sense at all, because Keti *didn't* feel that way.

But there had been something, well, disturbing about owning the brothels after that. It had bothered her.

So now she put all her efforts into the running of the reopened Empress Mine. But whenever she called Martin and suggested getting together, he always said, "Too busy. Don't have the time." Polite, aloof, shutting her out.

Nonetheless, he'd agreed to come to her Christmas party. Indeed, the whole Collins clan had accepted her invitation. And when Keti had met him at the door and welcomed him inside, Martin had greeted her politely. He'd given her a casual, rather distant hug, a hug that meant nothing. Because even within that brief contact, he had shut her out.

Still, she was the hostess. She couldn't afford to be thrown off by her disappointment, to be made miserable by it. Not now, anyway, but later perhaps.

She brought out mimeographed sheets of Christmas carol lyrics. "How about singing, everyone?"

Her guests took the pages, distributing them easily. Some went to the dining room for a refill of cider or wine or for more hors d'oeuvres and holiday sweets.

The house, Martin reflected, even *smelled* expensive. Yes, she had a tree, and he could smell the evergreen, yet there was also the spicy scent of Christmas potpourri and the pristine perfection of it all. It was not lived-in as, say, his parents' house, or his sister Bridget's house in Carson City was. Yet Keti Whitechapel lived here.

Keti, Keti, Keti. No longer the soft, caring creature who had met him outside the mine after her shift the year he'd returned from Vietnam; no longer that young woman who had been willing to show him her vulnerability. Keti *had* still had vulnerability back then.

Maybe she'd even had it that night at the brothel, the night the baby was born to the African woman whose name he couldn't remember.

Certainly, *something* had persuaded Keti to sell those businesses.

But she seemed completely invulnerable now. Now, Martin pitied her, and yet he also feared her.

She even looked expensive. Her hair and skin and body seemed a testament to the health and beauty that money could buy. She *must* still be the deep person he once had known, but that depth was hidden under a brittle facade. Or so it seemed to Martin. He longed for the woman she once had been. Or for the woman he'd hoped she might sometime decide to be.

As Bridget prepared to play carols on the piano, other guests gathered around. Martin moved toward the woman in the glorious sequined dress. It was long-sleeved and dipped low in the back, showing off her muscular body.

How to reach her. "You look beautiful," he said.

She lifted her face to see him, and she smiled, her mouth wide and voluptuous.

The old longing stirred within him, along with a knowledge that she could still be his—but only exactly as she was. Keti, successful investor, mine owner, ski resort tycoon.

She held out her song sheets, to share them with him.

Bridget said, "All right. Everyone sing. 'God Rest Ye Merry Gentlemen.'"

And Keti sang beside Martin, her familiar alto merging with his baritone.

"God rest ye merry gentlemen, let nothing you dismay; remember Christ our Savior was born on Christmas Day..."

Paul's boys, behind their uncle and Keti, held on to their song sheets but whispered with each other.

Keti had gifts for them, as for all Martin's family,

glossy wrapped packages that the boys hadn't opened yet. They would take them back to the Collins house when they left. Every year, Keti gave presents to each member of the Collins clan, as if they were her own family.

Which, Martin supposed, they were. The only family she had, barring Marlene, who wasn't here tonight, who was spending Christmas in London. No, Keti wasn't completely selfish. But Martin knew he couldn't live with her. If she was to be as she was, she must be separate from him. Life with *that* Keti, the Keti who really existed, wasn't what he envisioned for himself. If he were to have a lover, a wife, a partner—and he had considered such a thing, had known women he thought might fill the bill—then it would be someone different from Keti.

Different how?

When it came to that question, he faced the knowledge that he wanted Keti, Keti exactly, if only a little bit different.

And he'd had no lover other than her since Vietnam.

Nonetheless, the logical place for her in his life was this one—what they had now. She was a lifelong friend, a former lover, someone he might know into old age as a casual acquaintance.

He could not change her and he had no right to try.

And so they must be only what they were to each other.

He felt her attention on him, even though her gaze was resting on the lyrics they held. He watched her hands as she lifted the first sheet to reveal the second carol. How many years had they sung carols together, decorated his parents' tree together? There had been enough of them. Now, though, she was a stranger to him. Hardened and, he suspected, lonely.

Wasn't it important for him to help ease that loneliness? She'd called him and wanted to get together. He'd made excuse after excuse. Yes, his work kept him busy. But not too busy for a friendship.

I will try to be her friend, he vowed silently. Reminding himself that she wasn't his type and he was not tempted by her, and that their friendship would go nowhere that it shouldn't go.

"You're staying at your parents' tonight, then?" she asked, as they said good-night, after the extended Collins family and many other guests had departed.

"Tradition," he admitted. "Keti, if you want to get together—ski or something—I'd be glad to do that."

Keti studied his eyes, searching for something. *For love,* he thought. Well, what he had to offer was friendship.

She said, "Okay," and she seemed happy, happy that he had promised to spend time with her.

She needed his friendship.

Martin would give it. He owed her that.

Christmas Eve, Keti's thirty-eighth year

Fog drifted away from Keti's home, the beautiful home that was now a showplace. A Christmas Eve alone. No, not alone. Martin had invited Keti to join him at his parents' house this evening. His parents' house, where his mother lay dying of cancer.

Keti would go over, for a while, at least. Marlene was spending Christmas away again, this time in Monte Carlo, with a new husband. Marlene had invited her to join them for the holidays, but Keti had said, *Not this time.*

Keti would not leave Bounty now, not when Mrs. Collins might be taken from them at any time. It was not that she was particularly loving toward Martin's mother. But the Collins family had taken her in when she'd had no one else, and for that she would always be grateful.

So long ago.

I'm thirty-eight, Keti thought. Childless and unlikely to ever have children.

She'd wanted to have Martin's children.

Once.

She'd been a different person back then. Their love, when it was new, had made her idealistic. Now, she knew Martin as a realist. Yes, there was still some innocence about him—some kind of innocence. He was committed to his work, to endlessly helping all the families of Bounty.

Keti wasn't poor, would *never* be poor again, yet she knew she was one of his projects, as well.

He was always encouraging her to read, telling her about something he'd just discovered or a poem he'd found. He'd share these things whenever they got together for a hike or some skiing, which was at least twice a month.

Martin had become a friend to Keti, and over the years she had come to treasure his friendship more and more, even as she railed against the obvious reality that he no longer wanted her for a lover.

Keti's cars, both her pale yellow Mercedes convertible and the Hummer she'd bought earlier this year, were outside her house. But instead she decided to walk to the Collins place. It was five blocks away, and her walk home would be uphill. But, of course, Martin might drive her, too.

The snow fell softly as she stepped outside in her long winter coat with its fox-fur trim on the hood. She wore black wool pants that stretched snugly over her legs and rear end. The snow squeaked beneath her Sorel boots. A stray dog saw her but seemed to cower and back away when she stared at it. Keti was glad of that. She didn't like unfamiliar dogs and she wasn't crazy about those owned by acquaintances, either.

Many houses were decorated with the colorful lights of the season. At the Collins house, Mr. Collins had specially lit an elaborate nativity display that was mounted on the garage door.

With a heavy heart, thinking of Mrs. Collins lying so ill inside, Keti went up to the house and knocked.

Tiffany, who was now thirteen, opened the door. She had the look of, well, a kind of poverty. A frizzy perm, too much foundation and she was out of shape, especially for someone so young.

"Hello, Tiffany," Keti said. "How are you?"

Tiffany shrugged indifferently.

Like someone, Keti thought, with nothing to live for. Instead of someone with her whole life ahead of her.

Martin's father stepped through a doorway and exclaimed, "Why, hello, Keti!"

She embraced him. "How is Peggy?"

"She'll be glad you're here. She talks about you. She's been saying, 'There's something I must tell Keti.'"

Keti hadn't been to the Collins house all that much lately. It was winter, and she'd caught a cold. And then she'd had so much to do for work, plus there'd been a necessary trip to South Africa, to deal with some mining holdings there.

She hadn't been to see Peggy Collins for a week. But her abandonment of Martin's mother had a price.

She now realized it meant that much less time with her, the woman who was the closest thing to a mother Keti could remember.

Martin came out of his mother's room, the room where she'd been receiving hospice care for the past month. Her husband slept beside her when her pain allowed him to and in another bed in the same room when it did not.

"Keti," he said and immediately embraced her with one arm; in the other hand, he held a glass he'd just retrieved from his mother's room. "She wants to see you."

"Is she all right?" Keti asked, feeling stupid immediately afterward. Of course Mrs. Collins wasn't all right. She was dying of cancer.

"Soon," was all he said. "Go in."

Peggy Collins looked significantly worse—more tired, thinner, grayer, than she had just days before.

"Keti," she said.

The older woman seemed focused, however, when Keti came in and pulled out a chair by her bedside. She took Mrs. Collins's hand. The skin was pale, almost translucent, and the veins stood out. Keti said to her, "You're the only person like a mother I've ever known."

"I've often thought if Marlene could have come into your life earlier..." But Mrs. Collins didn't finish the sentence.

Keti said, "I'm surprised to hear you say that."

"Well, there's no need for you to be surprised," was the response, which meant, Keti thought, that Mrs. Collins wasn't about to criticize Marlene to Keti. "She loves you. I wouldn't have had you do some of the things she's encouraged you to do, but you make your own choices," Mrs. Collins added. The statement seemed to exhaust her.

Keti sat silently, holding her hand. "I did sell the brothels," she managed to say.

"Yes, and I was so...relieved." Mrs. Collins lay quiet for a moment. Then she said, "Martin loves you so."

"He loves his mother," Keti replied.

"Yes, but I don't think he even knows how much he loves you, Keti. When he is most angry, that's when I've seen it."

"He's a good man," Keti said. "He's been a good person the whole time I've known him. I'm not like that."

"But you're wonderful in your own way. We can't all be like Martin."

"He's *good*," Keti repeated. *Too good for me.* At least, it had seemed so to her for the past several years, especially whenever he'd distanced himself from her. The distancing was a subtle thing, and she'd tried to account for it, but Martin had a way of making it difficult to broach such a subject. If she said, *Martin, why are you avoiding me?*—or *Martin, why are you so distant from me?*—he simply denied that it was happening.

I'm as I always am, he would say.

And so Keti had gotten the message that he was done being physical with her, done being sexual with her, done being her lover.

She still didn't appreciate the message. Sometimes she had been so desperate for the attention of men that she had taken other lovers. But even when it was physically pleasurable, she couldn't help comparing the others to Martin, acknowledging that none could be as close to her as he was.

Keti wanted to ask his mother one thing now. "Do you think it's wrong, Mrs. Collins, that I like to make money?"

"Of course not." The other woman was thoughtful. "As long as you remember to love, as well. Money can be used for so many good things."

Keti thought, *Ah, money is different for her than it is for me. I think money is to be spent by those who've made it.* Though with discretion. And the poor should have something, yes. Enough. Didn't the government give them plenty, out of the pockets of people who'd worked hard? Yes, fringe benefits were for those who earned them. Keti could no longer imagine a moment in her future in which her fiscal well-being would ever be threatened. She'd managed to make her financial base diverse and impregnable. It would never fail.

She sat with the other woman in silence, waiting for whatever it was that Mrs. Collins still wanted to tell her.

"Keti."

"Yes."

"You mustn't isolate yourself. I can imagine how hard it is to be you. You must have people around you, true friends around you, always, Keti. Marlene won't live forever."

"Martin and I are friends."

Mrs. Collins looked as if she would have liked to say something more, but she held her tongue. Then, finally, she continued. "I think you saved him—after Vietnam. He was so disconnected when we first saw him at the hospital. Only when you came here with him for Christmas did I begin to believe he'd be all right."

"I would give Martin anything," Keti said at last. "But he won't take it from me."

"Don't you think perhaps that's what makes it impossible for him to be with you in the way both of you might like?"

"What do you mean?" Keti asked.

"It's hard for men to live on the earnings of women. For good men, that is."

"So, I should give up everything I have and be a housewife for Dr. Collins of Bounty," Keti blurted out before she could stop herself.

"You've grown hard, Keti."

"Why do people keep saying that? I've always been hard. As long as I can remember, anyway."

Mrs. Collins remarked, "It's been a gift to me to have you in our lives and in our home."

Keti couldn't see why. She said, "You took me in when I was so vulnerable. I'm where I am today because you invited me to live here with you."

Mrs. Collins had closed her eyes and appeared to rest.

Martin's mother died that night. All of the family were with her—all but Amy, of course, though maybe by now she and his mother were together again.

The funeral home had come for her body. It was 2:00 a.m. on Christmas Day. The Collinses were still awake, drinking wine in the living room, relieved and numb and sad.

Keti said, "My mother died on Christmas Day, too."

Martin glanced at her. He'd forgotten this, because Keti never talked about her mother, didn't remember her, had never known her.

He wanted Keti, and he recognized this impulse as a reaction to grief. Nonetheless, it felt like real need.

She would give herself to him, he knew. Keti was in love with him, just as she had been in love with him for years. She would always give him another chance and would always be willing to try again.

Sometimes Martin thought that the reason he was not living with her or married to her had something to do with a lack of nobility on his part. *I don't love her enough. I can't pretend to her that I love her as much as a man should love her.*

Undeniably, being with Keti was physical bliss. Physical.

Martin loved her, but he was no longer in love with her and he could not be anymore. Her lifestyle—so driven by money and possessions—repelled him. Somewhere along the road, he'd ceased to be in love and had begun to pity her instead.

He would not toy with Keti, no matter how much he wanted her comfort tonight.

She sat by the fire in her expensive clothes, with gold jewelry on her fingers and her ears, and with the watch he'd given her on her wrist.

She'd signed this year's package to him, "Love, your Scrooge."

And again he'd felt keen pity.

Martin was in love with life. Every day was a pleasure simply because he knew he could go outside and breathe mountain air and share life experiences with those around him.

Keti was different. She was so successful and yet she did *not*—as far as he could tell—particularly enjoy people. Martin had known mining culture, and he knew, too, about the effects of tailings, all the waste of mining, on the environment. He saw miners with silicosis in his practice. Keti would always make sure safety measures were observed, but that was primarily to protect herself, not her miners. And she also had holdings in South Africa, where Martin believed the workers were treated less well than they were in the United States.

He wasn't sure how he felt about the Bounty ski area, either. He skied there and he knew the patients in his practice did, too—those who could afford a season pass or at least a lift ticket. And yet Bounty had become affluent so suddenly—and at the same time it had become poor. In winter the streets were lined with the cars of wealthy visitors, there for the world-class ski runs. Whereas many of the locals lived in trailers and homes that were literally falling apart around them.

Keti had so much wealth, and she could do so much good with it if she wanted to.

Martin stopped the thought. He'd vowed long ago to quit trying to change Keti. She was who she was. She preferred a luxury hotel to a camping trip. She preferred shopping to an afternoon spent hiking or even skiing.

Yes, repellent, he thought again, looking at her and thinking that even her beauty had changed for him as it had become less and less natural, more and more expensive.

He would have liked to give her something she needed for Christmas. But there was nothing like that he could buy her, because she bought everything she needed and wanted for herself. He'd bought her a gift this year and hadn't liked himself for doing it because she *didn't* need it, might not even like it. He had yet to give it to her.

He stood up.

"Where are you going?" his father asked from his place by the fire. Surely, the older man was grappling with the hole that had just been made in their lives.

"Just outside. To look at the stars."

"I should go home," Keti said.

"You're welcome to stay," Martin's father told her.

"Thank you. I'd like to, but I didn't plan to leave the house for the night. I need to turn up the heat a bit to make sure the pipes don't freeze. I hate spending money on fuel," she added automatically.

"Your house *is* always cold," Tiffany agreed. The teenager was still awake, morosely paging through a magazine.

Keti said, "When you have to pay for propane, no doubt you'll appreciate the wisdom of putting on an extra sweater."

"That's the truth." Martin's father shook his head, half laughing, seeming lost.

"But you can afford to keep your house warm," Tiffany said.

Keti wanted to set her straight, but she held her tongue. Honestly. Somewhere along the line, Tiffany had failed to learn that the "rich" were rich *because* they made sacrifices, because they were careful with money. She sighed and turned away, thinking *Bah!* You couldn't tell anything to a girl like that. She hadn't been raised correctly and so she would end up worse off than her parents before her.

Martin said, "I'll walk you home."

"Thank you."

Keti asked Martin, "When will you have the funeral?"

"Probably in a few days. We'll have to allow enough time to let people come from farther away."

Their boots made identical squeaking noises on the snow. Keti noticed Martin was carrying a box under his arm. "Are we dropping that off somewhere?" she asked. Martin loved to leave surprise presents on people's doorsteps for them to find on Christmas morning. On the other hand, he had as yet given her no gift.

"Somewhere," he said and smiled at her.

Keti reflected that he bought gifts for her that he would never buy for himself. He bought nearly all his clothes secondhand. He lived frugally, ascetically, and so always had money to help other people. *We are polar opposites,* Keti thought. Yet it was Martin she wanted, Martin she loved.

Martin who might never again love her that way in return.

But she had tasted his love, and she could not forget it.

"How I wish," she told him, "that you still loved me as you used to."

He said, "Don't consider yourself unloved by me, Keti. Maybe it's better this way."

"How?"

"Maybe our love will last longer this way."

Our love. She heard those words and made herself believe in them. "Are you implying that if we'd done the normal thing and, say, gotten married, our love might have failed?"

"No." Clipped. Curt.

"Do you think we would have fought?"

"Doubtless." Somehow, she knew he would be smiling and she glanced up at him. Steam drifted lightly from his nose and mouth, from those sensual lips. She longed to touch the cleft in his chin, longed to feel the fine bones of his face beneath her fingertips.

She felt like a child beside him, wanting to ask, *Why? Why? Why?* Why couldn't they still be together as lovers, as partners, as one.

Lately, whenever she'd asked that question, he'd simply refused to answer.

He said, "I'll make you a deal, Keti."

"What?"

"Come and live with me at my house for one month as I live. You can work for me, too. Hell, you're certainly good with money. You can check out my bookkeeping. Take appointments for me. I'll find lots of things for you to do."

"What would that prove?"

"It would be instructive."

"How so? It wouldn't be real. I would know, all the time, that I had the financial security that you seem to find unimportant."

"You've never heard me say financial security is unimportant. But being a multimillionaire and being financially secure don't mean the same thing."

"They do to me."

Surprisingly, his gloved hand grasped hers, as if to comfort. "I know."

Kissing under the mistletoe that her decorator had hung for effect, Martin's lips parting, their tongues touching. "I have to go back home," he told Keti.

Yet she felt, through his body, that he wanted to stay.

It gave her hope, this awareness that he wanted her physically, at least.

"I'm going to take you up on your invitation," she said.

"What?"

"Living with you for a month."

"Ah." He put the box in her hands. "Here's your gift."

She looked at the small tag. *To Keti. Love, Martin.*

She removed the green ribbon, unwrapped the red plaid paper and opened the lid of the box. Inside were two things. A Norwegian sweater, which she knew hadn't come cheap because she'd tried on one like it in a local shop. And a book called *The Gift.*

"There are lots of ideas in it," he said. "Things we can talk about."

She tried on the sweater, which was red, white and black. She knew it would be her favorite piece of clothing, simply because it was from him. "Are you sure you don't want to stay?" She felt desperate as a woman in a Tennessee Williams play—Maggie "The Cat" trying to seduce Brick back to her bed.

"No. I'm sure that I *do* want to stay." He smiled and kissed her again. "But it would be for the wrong reasons right now."

"Such as…? That you want comfort because your mother has died? Martin, I want to comfort you."

He shook his head and detached himself from her hands.

Keti felt something within her dry up. And sorrow welled behind her eyes.

She could not show him her own misery right now, and gave him a bright smile instead. "Okay. See you sometime soon."

Chapter 8

Outside Martin's house

"I would like to skip this one," Keti tells Edith, knowing what is coming.

"But, Keti, this time *you* are the one who gives."

"I tell you I don't want to see it. I behaved stupidly, and I paid, and then I did something even stupider. I've paid again and again ever since. It was a terrible Christmas Eve."

"I don't think you really feel that way," Edith says, the child speaking as an adult, perhaps as the kind of wise angel she had become.

The Christmas Eve Keti was thirty-nine

There was no fog tonight. Only blinding snow, falling so deep and thick that Keti worried Martin's tires would merely spin without any traction.

"We have to go," Keti implored him, "and I don't think I can make it." Another spasm racked her body, and she could barely cope. It wasn't unbearable. But she had a feeling it might quickly become so. "I want to do it here."

"Not a good idea. Let's get to the hospital."

Keti was alone with Martin, and it was happening. The plan had been for him to be with her—before, during and after. If all went well, he would be able to deliver the baby at the hospital, though he wouldn't be the physician of record.

Again, she contemplated giving up the child she'd carried for thirty-nine weeks. Again, she "prepared" for that, as if there ever could be adequate preparation.

She would be with Martin. During the birth. And after, when she must leave the hospital without the child. She would go home to Martin's house. He'd even offered to stay with her at her place, if that was what she needed.

And she was relieved that she was going to the hospital.

She focused on two things. One, that the birth was beyond her control. This force taking control of her body was only growing stronger. Two, that she definitely wanted to get to Bounty's little hospital, where she'd planned to give birth. What if the baby got stuck? What if Keti needed a cesarean section?

She managed to get her coat and hat and mittens on, and Martin donned his parka and gloves.

This pregnancy should never have happened.

She couldn't give up this child, could she?

Yet how could she keep the baby?

Deceit, deceit… The truth itself would be painful, and it would lead to far more pain. Keti *must* grow up, must accept that Martin did not love her, not in the way that mattered most to Keti. He loved her the way that saints loved ordinary people. He didn't want her as his wife, as his partner.

Yes, they had tried to live together. To make it work. But there had been no making it work, and when Keti had realized it, when they had admitted it to each other, though after three months instead of just one, she'd felt angry and rejected—but also like an animal who'd been freed from a cage.

Though one final gambit of hers, a colossally stupid move, had resulted in this pregnancy. *Oh, and by the way, I stopped using birth control because I thought I wanted to have your baby.*

It was his baby. She had intentionally conceived Martin's child.

And now she could not keep it. Yes, she had the

money and means to support a child. But she just wasn't…motherly. And Martin did not love her. He would surely bind himself to her for the sake of the baby but never because of love for *her,* Keti. And she felt worse about all this than she ever had in her life, more stupid, selfish and worthless.

No, it's not yours, she'd told him, having taken off in a wild fashion after she'd moved out. She'd simply pretended… And he'd believed her. He must have *wanted* to believe her, she thought bitterly.

Oh, baby, I'm sorry. I'm sorry for everything.

"Careful, Keti. Watch the step here."

Martin guided her outside, down the snowy steps. If there'd been more time, she knew he would have shoveled them for her. But now they had to get to the hospital.

The snow whipped her and chilled her face to the bones. It wasn't just an ordinary blizzard but a raging arctic blizzard. For all that, she wasn't aware of the fierce cold. When Martin had helped her into the truck, she rolled down the window.

He got in and turned the key in the ignition.

Another contraction. She clutched Martin's arm. He waited. When she relaxed, he said, "It's not too late to change your mind. And I *will* marry you, Keti, if you want to keep this baby."

Yes, he'd said that already.

He would make this sacrifice so that she could

keep her child and so that the child would have a father in its life.

He would make the sacrifice even without knowing it was his child.

But marriage to her shouldn't *be* a sacrifice.

Her mind grappled with the thought that there was something wrong with her, that she would never marry or raise children of her own. She cared about money more than people, as Martin was fond of pointing out.

She shook her head.

He reminded her, "If you have a contraction, don't grab my arm while I'm driving."

"Yes," she agreed, gazing at that perfect chin of his, trying not to cry and wondering how she was going to get through all of this. What would she even do with a baby, if she were to keep it?

I can't.

She wondered if he was relieved by her response to his proposal. The only reason, *the only reason,* she would marry Martin was because he wanted to marry her. Because he wanted Keti Whitechapel for his wife.

And if he knew this was his baby, it would *really* be all about the baby.

God, what am I going to do?

Another contraction surged through her. She longed to lie down, to rest between these pains. At the hospital, she told herself, she could.

With Martin carefully steering a course down the road through the swirling, blowing snow, she felt strangely detached. Safe. The birth was beyond her control, and anyway, Martin was here. Martin wouldn't let her die.

He navigated with total focus, as if he were transporting something exceptionally precious.

The baby he thought wasn't his.

Keti had never known such pain, and she wished the nurses would quit asking if she wanted anything for it. All she could imagine was that it must hurt so much because something was wrong with the baby or its position, but everyone said that wasn't the case. Head down, just the way he should be. Or she.

Could a baby split a woman in two? This must be happening to her. She was going to die. She stood beside a bed in the maternity suite. They would take her to the delivery room soon, surely.

They'd wanted to put an electronic fetal monitor on her, but Keti had said she couldn't bear to stay flat on her back.

Pain relief she wanted, but she wasn't going to give in. She wasn't!

Martin held her arms as she lowered herself to her knees and clutched a chair for support.

She hated the gown split up the back, but somehow she'd almost forgotten about it. All she could think was that she was dying, dying in a hospital, and no one was doing a thing about it.

A nurse came in, took one look at her and said, "I think we need to get you into delivery."

It was good to push the baby out, but it hurt more than she could ever have imagined.

"You can push," said the doctor again, Martin's colleague. She'd only met him twice before this. And here he was now, away from his family on Christmas Eve. No, it was Christmas now. Martin had told her.

With this push she cried out, and then experienced an enormous sense of release. A release that felt disastrous.

Martin caught the baby, but Keti couldn't bear to look, to see him or the child. *If I look, it will be all over. I'll tell him the truth.*

The minutes passed, and they took the baby away to be cleaned up, saying Keti wasn't quite done. The placenta still had to come out. Martin's partner tried to show the infant to her, though. They said the baby was a girl. Keti glanced at it because she couldn't stop herself. *Oh, God. Oh, God. What have I done? What am I doing? I can't go through with this.* The newborn was tiny and purplish-red and infinitely... Keti didn't know how to define the creature; she only knew that she was amazed and that she must look no more. She turned her head away, shaking her head. *Martin's baby. Martin's daughter.*

Keti had decided what was right for her, and more important, right for this child.

A baby cannot make Martin love me in the right way. This is all so horrible, and I'm doing the wrong thing, but if I tell him the truth now... The result would be disaster. The loss of all his esteem.

Determined to look no more, she waved the doctor away.

A man's arm wrapped around her shoulders. Martin had pulled down his mask. "I'll be with you," he said. "But be sure, Keti. Be very sure."

How can I be sure of anything? she wanted to shout.

She didn't know anything except that she'd made a decision and she was going to stand by it. A couple from Fort Collins was waiting for this baby. They were already in town, although not at the hospital. Everyone wanted to be certain that Keti had made up her mind.

Why did it feel as if her limbs and her lifeblood were vanishing on her, as if she were being torn to pieces?

I hate myself—and I'll hate myself if I keep this child.

Martin did not let her go. She found her cheek wet—but not from her tears.

The tears were his.

Another Christmas, sometime later

Fog eddies around the foundation of an unfamiliar stone house. Keti, with Marley beside her, studies the street, the sidewalks, the snow-covered logs, the eaves dripping with Christmas lights.

"I don't know this place," she murmurs.

"That's true," Edith answers. "Come on, Keti. You must see who lives here."

"Is this…now?" she asks, trying to guess the year from the look of things around her.

"No. Not yet. It's about ten years ago."

The brunette in the red wool pants and matching sweater was stout. That's what Keti would call her. Her hair was graying, and she'd tied it back in a ponytail. The man, undoubtedly her husband, was a few years older.

The young girl was maybe six.

She was brunette.

Her eyes were brown.

Her nose was straight.

Her chin was like Martin's.

"Just one?" the little girl said, walking around the tree and looking at the small pile of presents. "I can only open one? Santa will bring more, won't he?"

And her birthday would be the next day. Surely, they would give her *something* for her birthday.

"You think that old fat man's going to bring you something, Charlotte?" teased the father.

The girl, Charlotte, bit her lip. She wanted an American Girl doll, the one named Kirsten, more than anything. She wanted her mother to sew clothes for her doll, and Charlotte could knit a scarf for the girl—she was learning to knit, and her older sister would help her if she got stuck.

But a full-size American Girl doll was expensive. Charlotte's parents didn't generally give her as many presents as some of her friends got. She walked around the tree, studying each package that was labeled for her. Finally, she picked the largest. It looked big enough. "This one," she said.

Her father smiled and turned away slightly.

Her mother nodded and sat down to watch.

Charlotte carefully unwrapped the paper—no tearing away gift wrap for this child. Then, her small hands pried open the lid.

There it was. Kirsten, in her box. She said, "You got her for me! She's just what I wanted!"

Both parents beamed at her. Sometimes they might seem stern, but they saw her as their treasure.

One night seems to blend into another, and Keti recognizes yet another Christmas—her last Christmas with the Collins family.

* * *

Martin parked his truck outside Keti's Victorian.

He walked up to the stately house and rang the doorbell, listening to it chime.

Heels clacked on the tile of the foyer inside, and the door swung open.

Keti, in a red Donna Karan suit with Jimmy Choo boots and her blond hair in a smooth pageboy. She seemed more distant from Martin than ever before.

"There you are," she said.

Martin stepped inside.

Keti murmured a hello, but she seemed scarcely to see him. "I'm ready," she said with a shrug, "whenever you are."

She lifted an expensive camel-hair coat from the staircase railing and began to slip it on. Then she handed Martin a tin of Pepperidge Farm Christmas cookies from the hall table.

"What are these for?" he asked.

She shrugged again. "Fluffany."

"*Why* do you call Tiffany that?"

"Because she *is* fluffy. All fluff and no common sense."

"Ah." And then Martin noticed that Keti, the woman who had everything she needed and so much more besides, had no actual gift packages anywhere in sight.

Just a tin of cookies.

He blushed for her, and felt shame just as if *he* were the one who had been so selfish.

The house in Bounty, at the present time

Keti awakes in her bed and realizes she has been crying. Had she dreamed all of that? Obviously. But what strange and vivid dreams they had been.

That child, the girl to whom she'd given birth, the girl she could now almost make herself forget was Martin's daughter, too, should be sixteen this Christmas. Keti doesn't know the names of the people who adopted her. She doesn't know *her* name, her daughter's name. Though in the dream she had been called Charlotte.

And in her dream, Keti was allowed to see her as a happy child. If she could believe the dream.

And, oh, that strange bit about Edith.

She turns on a light and looks toward the mirror.

Something moves beside her, and she jumps. Marley, of course. The dog's pale eyes are open and he's watching her. Marley thumps his short tail and gazes at her.

Poor, starved thing, she thinks.

Then, she marvels to herself, *I have a dog. How did it happen that I have a dog?*

She knows perfectly well. Marley made it clear that he needed Keti; that she had to help him.

"You're better for me than any lesson a spirit of Christmas could bring, Marley. Did you have funny dreams, too?" she asks.

It's hard to tell from Marley's expression.

She can see herself now in Aunt Marlene's mirror. Remembering the envelope and the photos, she gets up to retrieve them. Perhaps one of them will be of her aunt. How did Marlene come to have those childhood pictures of her and Martin? Keti wonders. Then, she remembers. One year, when Marlene came to the Collins house, the Collinses gave her a photo album filled with pictures of Keti. Pictures they'd taken of the Collins children when they'd been playing with Keti, before she'd come to live with the family, had been included, as well.

Keti pulls the photos from the envelope.

There's Martin again, Martin and Keti, Martin that Christmas after he'd come home from Vietnam. Ah, and here is a shot of Keti and Marlene at the Palomino Palace. A Christmas party.

Marlene died alone.

It had just happened that way—a massive stroke. One of the girls found her.

The state police had explained all this to Keti.

She remembers her dream—it *must* have been a dream, vivid as it seemed. But Marlene with her handcuffs, Marlene in her red suit, Marlene ancient and trapped... *My dear aunt. You must be happy now, wherever you are, wherever the dead are. I don't believe there could have been a vile judgment for you in the end.*

What do I believe? Keti wonders.

She supposes she is an atheist—or something like that. And yet…

She shivers, walking herself through those strange dreams again. She remembers the kindness of the Collins family. She thinks about Martin's determination to give to others.

He isn't judgmental these days. But he still holds himself aloof from Keti. *As if he might catch something. Greed.* Granted, his face lights up with a bright smile whenever he sees her. But she wonders if the only way he knows of to be friends with her is to detach himself utterly. Because how she believes she must live is so different from how he would live if he were in her position.

She sets the photos on her night table and turns out the light. She remembers the little girl, Charlotte.

If I were to make a Christmas wish…

A single wish.

But life has taught her that the only thing she can count on is what she does for herself.

Is that what I've learned? she wonders.

Or is it only what she's practiced?

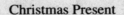

Christmas Present

Chapter 9

Christmas present

Sitting up in bed, Keti has no need to be told that the church bell is again striking one. The air feels different. All that wasn't a dream, was it? Because she believes that she has been restored to consciousness just in the nick of time, for the special purpose of meeting with the second messenger dispatched to her through Aunt Marlene's intervention.

Beside her, Marley sighs and rolls onto his side.

Lying down again, Keti takes a sharp look all around the bed. For she wishes to challenge her

visiting spirit on the moment of its reappearance.
She does not intend to be taken by surprise.

But nothing happens.

The first visitor—Edith—was just a part of a
dream, after all. Well, isn't that what Keti told
herself? Why is she expecting something so absurd
as a second spirit?

She turns over and pets the dog, and Marley licks
her face. His breath is surprisingly nice. For all his
malnourishment, he must have good teeth.

"Just a dream, Marley. I wish you could talk. You
could tell me *your* dreams."

But a light has just appeared. A light coming from
the mirror, perhaps, but suffusing everything with its
glow. Yes, the source and secret of this ghostly light
must be the mirror. This idea taking possession of
Keti's mind, she gets up softly and slips to the end of
the bed, toward the mirror. Marley sits up, too. He
sniffs.

Keti smells it, too. Food.

"Marley," she cries softly, afraid to be separated
from the dog. He comes toward her. Sniffing.

And now it's as if the mirror surrounds them and
they are in another part of the house. They're downstairs, in the living room. Yes, it's Keti's own house.
There is no doubt about that. But it has undergone a
surprising transformation. The walls and ceiling are
so hung with evergreen boughs, that it looks a perfect

grove, from every part of which bright, gleaming berries glisten. Crisp leaves of holly, mistletoe and ivy reflect the light, as if so many small mirrors have been scattered there; and such a mighty blaze roars in the fireplace, as that dull petrification of a hearth has never known in Keti's time or for many a season gone.

But that's not the strangest part.

There's no keeping Marley at her side. What sits before them seems the starving dog's personal Christmas gift.

Heaped upon the floor, to form a kind of throne, are turkeys, geese, game, poultry, great joints of meat, long wreaths of sausages, pies, puddings, barrels of oysters, red-hot chestnuts, cherry-cheeked apples, juicy oranges, luscious pears, immense cakes and seething bowls of cider, all making the chamber dim with their delicious steam. Reclining upon a sofa is a figure, no skinny waif. She's all round curves, and it's Amy Collins, happy, joyful, glorious to see. She bears a glowing torch, in shape not unlike Plenty's horn, and she holds it up, *high* up, to shed its light on Keti.

"Hello, Keti."

Though Amy's eyes are clear and kind, Keti's reluctant to meet her gaze. *I'm terrified,* she thinks.

"I am the Ghost of Christmas Present," says Amy with a grin.

Amy wears a simple deep green robe bordered

with white fur. The garment hangs loosely on her. Beneath the robe she wears nothing; even her feet are bare; and on her head she wears a holly wreath, set here and there with shining icicles. Her dark brown curls are long and free, free as her genial face, her sparkling eyes, her open hands, her cheery voice, her unconstrained demeanor and joyful air. Girded round her middle is an antique scabbard, but there's no sword in it, and the ancient sheath is eaten up with rust.

Keti can only stare.

Amy rises, seeming altogether on a larger scale than she ever did in life. She's giant, really.

"Amy," says Keti submissively, "let's get this over with. I went with Edith because she compelled me to, and I've learned a lesson. If you have anything more to teach me, I'd like to profit by it."

"Touch my robe!" says Amy.

Keti does as she's told and holds fast.

Turkeys, geese, game, poultry, meat, sausages, pies, puddings, oysters, chestnuts, apples, oranges, pears, cakes, cider, even the elk leg Marley is working on, all vanish instantly. Marley barks sharply, then lies down with a dejected whimper, and the room, the fire, the glow and the hour of night disappear, as well.

They stand on Main Street in downtown Bounty on Christmas morning. There are people here and they make a rough but not brisk and not unpleasant kind of noise, scraping snow from the pavement in front of those shops open even on this day, as skiers walk past with their equipment over their shoulders.

The sky is gloomy and the streets are choked with a thick mist, whose heavier particles descend in a shower of sooty atoms, as if all the hearths in Nevada had, in a single moment, been laid with fires and were now blazing away to their hearts' content. There's nothing particularly cheerful in the climate or the town, and yet there's an air of cheerfulness abroad that the clearest summer air and brightest summer sun might not have produced.

For the people shoveling, others headed for the slopes, even those opening shops and coffeehouses for the benefit of the tourists, are gleeful, calling out to one another. The market is open, its windows painted with holiday scenes, and Keti peers inside at aisles overflowing with fruit and vegetables.

There are the churchgoers, too, hustling toward one or another of Bounty's three churches. The long coats of the women—camel hair, fur, bright, rich wools—stand out like splendid ornaments against the snowy landscape. Children run ahead and behind in their Christmas finery, and the men are proud and pleased.

At the same time, innumerable more ordinary-looking people emerge from the side streets, carrying their breakfasts with them. Keti recognizes the

Mexican man who cleared her front walk the night before, and others… Well, there are some poor people in Bounty.

The sight of these people seems to interest Amy very much, for she stands with Keti and Marley beside her in the doorway of a bakery, sprinkling some sort of incense on their dinners from her torch. It's an uncommon kind of torch, for once or twice when there are angry words between some of the passersby who have accidentally jostled each other, she sheds a few drops of liquid on them from it, and their good humor is restored at once. They say that it's a shame to quarrel on Christmas Day.

They walk on, the three of them, Amy, Keti in her nightgown and bare feet never feeling the ice and snow, and Marley. They are invisible to those around them, Keti decides, for no one seems to notice them. Notwithstanding Amy's immense presence, she accommodates herself to any place with ease; she stands gracefully beneath a low roof, just as she would in the loftiest hall.

Keti isn't surprised when she sees where Amy eventually leads her.

Out to the end of town where the trailer park is, the trailer park that's packed to capacity, the trailers a mere six feet apart.

Tiffany, Amy's daughter and Keti's goddaughter,

lives here, with her four children and also the father of the youngest child.

Christmas Present with the Collins family

Martin hardly had to knock at the door of Tiffany's trailer before his niece opened it and exclaimed, "Hi, Uncle Martin!

"Martin's here!" she called to the others.

Tiffany was blond these days, her hair wiry from its latest perm, and Martin wasn't sure anymore what her hair would look like in its natural state. She was wearing tight hip-huggers, and some of her bulk spilled over the waistband underneath her red sweater, which had a Christmas tree appliquéd on the front.

Martin hugged his niece, while holding on to the bags of gifts he'd brought with him.

"Come on in!" Tiffany exclaimed, smiling broadly. "Oh, I hear Tim. I better see to him."

Her youngest child had been named Timothy, for his father. Quite a departure, Martin always thought, from Athena, Chaparral and Crazy Horse—the names of Tiffany's older children. Crazy Horse was only four, and Martin expected that noble name to metamorphose into something else pretty quickly once he hit kindergarten. On the other hand, Crazy Horse liked his name.

But as for Tim, their own Tiny Tim, there was

something wrong with him, which seemed to be the result of a long and difficult birth. He'd had a heart operation immediately after birth, hadn't walked at all until he was two and he still wasn't speaking at three. But his brother and sisters fought to be the one to hold him and push him in a stroller or pull him in a wagon.

Tim Senior, Tiffany's husband, entered the foyer with a can of Budweiser in hand. "Hi, Martin. How about a beer?" His forearms were covered with tattoos, and his gray hair hung past his shoulders and, as usual, was tied in a ponytail. Martin liked Tim, who fixed motorcycles for a living and rode them as a vocation.

As Martin followed him into the living room, where a small tree stood in the corner beside a television set showing the football game of the day, Martin's niece, Chaparral, hurled herself at him. "Martin, build me a snow fort."

Martin's father rose from his seat in front of the television. He'd sold the old Collins house after his wife's death and bought the trailer next door to Tiffany's. Then he'd given her the money to buy this one, and had settled the balance of Bridget's credit card bills, which she had promptly run up again.

Martin and his father embraced. Mr. Collins's eyes were still bright, the whites as clear as they always had been. Tiffany's oldest daughter, Athena, set the table at the end of the room closest to the kitchen, using a green tablecloth that had been in the family for years. Martin smelled spices and a turkey cooking and he went into the kitchen to hug his sister Bridget and Bridget's oldest daughter, as well as her infant. As Tiffany checked on the turkey, Bridget's younger daughter agreed to build Chaparral and Crazy Horse the snow fort they wanted. When Martin lifted pot lids on the stove, Bridget and Tiffany hissed at him to keep out of the food. Then Tiffany relented and offered him a taste of the yams and stuffing as he picked up his nephew Tim from a seat in the corner of the tiny kitchen.

Thin and underdeveloped, Tim still needed to be seen by a host of specialists, and Martin had done everything he could to make this happen. Tiffany had learned, in California, of a French specialist who was having great success with various physical and mental exercises for late-developing children. So now Martin was trying to figure out a way for Tiffany's son to see the man.

The bell sounded again, and soon the trailer was full, with the arrival of Paul and his family. Then George appeared, at last, with his military haircut. George was career military, which was something Martin didn't discuss with him. Nothing he'd seen in Vietnam had made him believe in the service. So he simply embraced his brother and told him he looked great, which he did.

"He got the looks for the whole family," Bridget said.

"Uncle Martin's not half-bad, either," Tiffany remarked. "Can one of you guys get the kids from outside?"

Martin thought of Keti, regretting her absence. Most other years, he'd been able to persuade her to be near them at Christmastime. Not this one, however.

He'd hurt her feelings, and they were estranged. Last year, he'd made it clear that he didn't want to be lovers, even occasional lovers, anymore. And then he'd foolishly mentioned the tin of cookies, which was all she'd brought to Tiffany's. Bringing that up had made *him* feel clumsy, ungentlemanly and worse; and it had made Keti cry, something that surprised him.

The situation still ate at him. It disturbed Martin that he should love someone so...selfish. It bothered him that he couldn't accept her as she was. Most of all, it nearly destroyed something inside him to watch her grow harder every year, less and less concerned for the people all around her, those who worked for minimum wage or less and those who had no employment at all. How had this happened to *Keti?*

As they sat down at the table, his father said, "You

know, I still feel so used to having Keti here for Christmas dinner."

"Keti Whitechapel has never been *here* in this trailer except once, last year, when she decided not to bring anything," Tiffany said sharply. "I can do just fine without having her name mentioned today."

Martin eyed her in surprise as he placed his napkin in his lap.

"Let's say grace," Bridget suggested, and Mr. Collins led them all in giving thanks before they launched into their meal.

"I invited her," Tiffany continued. "And by the way, you should see the inside of that house these days—well, I suppose you have, but not lately. Catch her having a party. It would cost her something. The house is worth, I don't know, a couple million dollars, I bet. Maybe more. All the beds have fabulous mattresses and beautiful imported sheets, and no one ever sleeps there but her."

Martin's throat swelled shut, and he saw Keti's face in his mind, her smile with the chipped tooth that she'd never had capped. He remembered a younger Keti, when her expression was still vulnerable. Now, she had the face of a porcelain figure, frozen in time. Hard.

"Her mother died on Christmas," he said, as if that could be a defense for Keti's ungenerous behavior.

"She doesn't love anyone," Tiffany continued. "She's like a robot."

"Not really, she's not," Martin said. Though Keti had taken other lovers, he suspected that he was the only one who had ever touched her heart. And he knew that she loved him still, might always love him. He felt responsible because of that, helpless to stop it or to cure her of her love for him.

Quite sure that he didn't want to cure her.

Her aunt Marlene had died earlier this year, too, and now Keti was utterly without blood relatives.

Then there was the wound of giving up that infant girl… Keti had never questioned what she'd done, and always said she was certain it had been the right choice.

Or at least that was what she said to him.

Martin didn't like to think about that child, that birth, the suspicions he'd had then, his acceptance of what Keti had told him.

Despite what his heart and eyes and reason had whispered. No, shouted…

He couldn't look too closely at why—at any of the whys. Things he'd seen in Vietnam. Things he'd done. Parts of his character and his past he'd never examined because to do so might well open a door to self-hatred.

Where is she? he wondered. *Where is Keti today? How will she react if I call her?*

"Anyway," Tiffany continued, "she's just one of those rich people who thinks only about herself."

"Thank you, Tiffany," Mr. Collins said firmly.

And now Bridget looked up and said, "I'm sorry for her."

Martin nearly left the table, knowing how Keti would react to Bridget's pity.

Tiffany said, "*Why?* She's got everything she ever wanted. She practically owns all of Bounty."

"I'm truly sorry for her," Bridget continued. "I couldn't be angry with her if I tried. Who suffers from her choices? Keti, always. She has taken it into her head not to be with us, for whatever reason, and she won't come and dine with us. What's the consequence?"

"She loses a great dinner!" exclaimed Paul's wife. Everybody else said the same.

"But the real issue," Bridget said, "is that the consequence of her taking a dislike to us, or to Martin—" she added with a meaningful look at her brother "—is that she loses some pleasant moments, which could do her no harm. I am sure she loses much more happiness than she'd be likely to find amid her own thoughts, either in that huge, empty house or at her desk at the mine. If I have my way, we'll keep asking her to join us every year. She must bear us, every Christmas, saying, 'Keti, how are you? Please be with us.' And maybe, as a result, she'll at least leave a generous tip for a maid in a hotel somewhere or maybe be more lenient toward some of her employees in South Africa. And *that* would be something."

They lingered over dinner, talking and laughing, getting up to go out for a short walk together before dessert. Afterward, they returned to the trailer for pie and brownies and cider and carols.

"Deck the halls with boughs of holly
Fa-la-la-la-la la-la-la-la
Tis the season to be jolly..."

Martin sat with Tim on his lap, singing gently to the boy, and Tim tried to sing, too, but it wasn't coherent. Still, they were all proud of him.

Next came Charades, and then everyone joined in Twenty Questions.

When it was his turn, Tim Senior held his own through a brisk fire of questioning. He was thinking of an animal, a live animal, rather a disagreeable animal. An animal that sniffed and occasionally snapped, and lived in Bounty and drove rather than walked... Each question had him laughing harder, and at a certain point Martin rose, with his nephew in his arms, and walked into the kitchen to get another brownie. He'd worked out the answer already, and saw Athena falling on the floor laughing, crying, "It's Keti Whitechapel!"

"She's given us plenty of merriment," said Mr.

Collins, not altogether happily. He lifted his glass of cider. "But I'd prefer to drink to her health. To Keti, who is still our friend."

Martin reached for a glass of water beside the sink and raised it. "Hear, hear!"

"A Merry Christmas and a Happy New Year to Keti," Bridget agreed. "She won't take the wish from us, but may she have both, nonetheless."

Keti and Amy, later the same night

Keti and Marley and the ghostly Amy are no longer at Tiffany's trailer. Amy is taking them to another trailer, instead. A huge Mexican-American family, twenty-three people celebrating together, in a rented home that is clean but has a hole in one door, put there by some other tenant in the past. For all that, the people inside embrace each other with beatific smiles. Children are lifted high in the air. Keti thinks she recognizes the faces of a couple of the miners who work in the Empress Tunnel.

"Feliz Navidad!"

And out to the streets again, where people are rushing from one home to another. Keti is remembering Martin holding little Tim, Tiffany's youngest, and she thinks about his gentleness and acceptance, his love of the child, which is so simple and pure.

It is dark now. Such a long night, if it is only a

night, or even just an hour, because the Christmas holidays appear to have been condensed into the brief space of time she and Amy have spent together.

Still, Amy is growing older, clearly older, and somehow her hair has turned gray.

"What is happening to you, Amy?" Keti asks.

"My life in this form is very brief," she replies. "It ends tonight."

"Tonight!" cries Keti, clinging to Marley's collar and checking the dog to make sure he isn't aging, too. But, no, he's the same and he has found a bone, probably belonging to one of the trailer park dogs, which he is carrying happily. She glances at the aging Amy and notices something sticking out from under the hem of her robe. "Is that a claw?" Keti exclaims in horror.

"It might be, for all the flesh on it. Look." From the foldings of the garment, Amy brings out two children—wretched, abject, frightful, hideous and miserable. They kneel at her feet and cling to the fabric that enfolds her.

Keti sees a boy and a girl. Yellow, meager, ragged, scowling, wolfish and yet humble. Instead of showing all the natural beauty of the young, a stale and shriveled hand has pinched and twisted and pulled their countenances to shreds. Devils lurk within the two and glare out menacingly. No change, no degradation, no perversion of humanity through all the mysteries of creation has monsters half so horrible, Keti thinks.

She starts back, appalled. She tries to say they are fine children, but the words choke her and she cannot voice the lie.

"Are they yours?" she finally asks.

"They are mankind's," Amy explains sadly. "This boy is Ignorance and the girl is Want. Beware them both, but most of all beware the boy. On his brow, I see written, Doom, unless the writing can somehow be erased."

"Don't they have somewhere to go, someone to care for them?"

"The government gives them what they need." Amy echoes words Keti has often used. She shrugs, just as Keti shrugs.

Then the church bell chimes.

One.

Two.

Amy is gone, and Keti and Marley are alone on their own street. When Keti lifts her eyes again, she beholds a phantom, draped and hooded, coming like a mist along the ground.

Coming directly toward her.

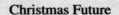

Christmas Future

Chapter 10

This third phantom is wrapped within a deep black garment, which shrouds its head, its face, and its form, and leaves nothing visible but one outstretched hand.

Its presence fills Keti with dread, and Marley whimpers and leans against Keti's pajama-clad legs.

"Do you represent Christmas Yet to Come?" Keti asks. It must be so, she imagines, as Dickens once described it. What happened, Keti wonders, to make these strange dreams come to her? Nothing has happened to her but the mirror. All Christmas Eve Day, she scarcely spoke to anyone about anything other than business. It had been a day much like any other.

Now she feels icy. Not her skin, not her flesh, but *inside,* everywhere, as if she is made of ice.

Keti tries once more, saying, "Will you show me things that haven't happened yet but *will* happen?"

The ominous figure nods once.

It does not speak, and Keti finds she is too cold to shiver. When she tries to walk, her legs tremble, yet in a brittle way, and she begins to wonder if she has actually died and if this is death. She is so cold, so cold. The spirit pauses to wait.

Keti says, "Ghost of the Future, I fear you more than the ghosts of Edith and Amy. But I believe your purpose is to do me some good. Won't you at least say something?"

Nothing. Its hand points straight before them.

Keti recognizes the mine office where she works. It's daylight now, and a couple of her employees, one searching a file drawer, another seated at her computer, are working frantically as if they are trying to sort out something of critical importance. A woman, one of the women miners, stands in the office doorway and has just asked the others a question.

Keti's employee at the computer never looks up from the screen. "I don't know much about it either way. I only know she's dead."

"When did she die?" asks the woman.

"Last night, I believe."

"What was the matter with her, anyhow?" asks the man who is rummaging through a filing cabinet. He is Keti's personal assistant, Jason. "I thought she'd never die."

"God knows." The man at the computer yawns.

The woman miner leans on Keti's desk—something that Keti would *never* allow. "So what'd she do with her money? That's what I want to know. Does she have any heirs?"

"If so, I'm not one of them," Jason replies. "But apparently there's not going to be a funeral. I mean, who would go?"

The phantom glides on, into the gray day, over icy, snow-covered ground. Keti recognizes a familiar landmark. It's the Palomino Palace sign.

But I don't even own that place anymore.

She wants to point this out to the phantom, but clearly she's supposed to observe rather than comment.

The women who work there are inside. It's early morning, a lull between customers. A prostitute Keti remembers is named Jackie drags on her cigarette from her seat on a vinyl couch near the bar. "Guess who died?"

Blond Cindy, the smallest and youngest prostitute in the house, looks up.

Jackie starts singing, "Ding! Dong! The witch is dead!"

"No way!" gasps another of the girls.

But by then others have taken up the chorus. They link arms, then parade through the establishment, cheering and singing joyfully.

Keti gladly follows the phantom away from this, and her apprehension increases.

They are no longer in Nevada.

Now they are in New York and two women investors whom Keti knows well stand talking outside Saks. "How are you?" asks one.

"Oh, great. And you?"

"Well, the old bitch got her comeuppance at last."

"So I heard. Oh, look at those fantastic pumps!" Together, the women head into the store.

Not another word.

Keti wonders why the phantom is showing her this trivial conversation. But finally it dawns on her, and she thinks back to the scene at the brothel. *They're all talking about me!*

Ghastly.

Well, inevitably one day she would die.

She follows the phantom into darkness and fog, Marley close beside her. Yes, this looks like Bounty. Where are they?

Oh, beside the free box, which Keti would gladly have burned before now. The Bounty free box, where wealthier residents leave unneeded garments and belongings, simply *attracts* poor people like a magnet. Including people who have no business being poor. Like that young man out of college, white and undoubtedly from an upper middle-class background, but with a completely untrimmed beard, bare feet, and worst of all, *dreadlocks*. With him is a young woman wearing a giant tam covering all her hair, and they have *children* with them, too.

"What did you get?" asks the woman, peering over the man's shoulder.

"A laptop."

Keti recognizes *her* laptop, a model owned by no one else in Bounty.

The young woman retrieves a cashmere coat and pulls it on. "You know, they just tossed all this here. She doesn't have a single heir, did you know that?"

"Doesn't surprise me," he answers. "No one liked her."

Keti is chilled. *It is me. I'm the one who died. Maybe I'm dead now.*

She's about to learn if that is true, too, because she well recognizes the next stop. Hadn't she come here after Amy died, and after Mrs. Collins's death, as well? It is the Holly Funeral Home.

The funeral director is nowhere in sight. Just…remains. An elderly man stretched out on one table. And on the other…

I don't want to see! I don't want to see!

It is Keti, middle-aged and dead. She doesn't remember dying. But that is her. No makeup. Of course not. She's to be cremated.

I'm dead. I'm dead!

"Is there any person," she asks the ghost, "who is sorry I'm dead?"

There's a whirl of fog, and then she is at Tiffany's trailer.

She's not sorry, **Keti** thinks.

The Collins family is assembled inside. Keti sees Martin standing staring out a window, toward the trailer next door. Keti searches the house and sees only Collins relatives.

Tiffany has a black eye under her makeup, and Tim, her husband, is in front of the television, paying no heed to the children. He is drinking, and Tiffany whispers to Bridget, "If Keti hadn't seized the land the shop was on… He was never like this when he could *work*."

Bridget nods solemnly.

Mr. Collins has heard them, and his mouth forms a grim line.

But nobody says—yet—that they are glad she is dead.

This is a nightmare, a horrible nightmare, Keti thinks.

Martin comes into the kitchen.

"We were just talking about your favorite person," Tiffany says.

Martin swallows.

"You're probably the only person in all of Bounty," his niece continues, "who cares that she's dead."

"Unfortunately," his father says, "she died a long time ago, while she was still walking this earth."

"Yes," Martin manages to say, and he walks into the other room and out into the darkness. No tears, no more words, yet Keti feels his grief for her, and feels the weight of all those disappointed hopes he had for her.

And then she is outside her house, which is up for sale.

For sale. Because I'm dead.

With no one to scatter her ashes.

With no tombstone that anyone would visit, if they could.

The phantom is still with her.

"Can't I change this?" she asks. "Is it too late?"

No answer.

She finds herself begging. "Intercede for me. Help me, please. This isn't who I ever meant to be, but I've never believed I could be different. It wasn't safe to be like Martin—or that man who shoveled my walk. Like ordinary people. It was never safe! But safety *isn't* the most important thing. You've proved that." And Keti catches the spectral hand and will not let go. If this horrible creature is the only one who can help her...

Yet the phantom vanishes.

The spectral hand becomes a bedpost, in her darkened room. A furry head shifts to lean against her, and she feels a rough tongue on her face.

"Marley." She hugs the dog.

Oh, thank God! This is her room, in her house, and she is *alive,* not dead.

And she has been given another chance.

Suddenly, there is no time. But not in the sense that there has been no time before this—no time for anything but work. Now, there's no time to do all the things Keti wants to do before Christmas Day begins.

The Spirit of Christmas

Chapter 11

Christmas Day
Bounty

Martin awoke before it was light. Because the old family home had been sold, he'd spent Christmas Eve in his own house. Of course, his father had extra room in his trailer, and all the Collinses were used to camping out on the floors, occupying every inch of carpet in the two side-by-side trailers. But often Martin worked on Christmas, and on those occasions it was simply easier to be in his own home.

He thought of Keti in her huge, lonely mansion, her beautiful house, no doubt waking up alone on Christmas Day. Later on, he'd call her—and he'd answer the other call, which had been left on his machine the night before. "This is Melanie Grady. I'm visiting Bounty and staying at the Hot Springs Motel, and it's imperative I speak with you. I'd rather wait to say what it's about when I see you."

Martin knew no Melanie Grady. Yet the phone call had convinced him to put off heading over to Tiffany's until he'd spoken with this person. It could be someone wanting to know about the new low-income medical clinic he was trying to get started in Bounty.

When he'd approached Keti about the idea, she'd said, "I thought your practice *was* a low-income clinic." So, he'd been trying to interest other regional philanthropists. It wasn't out of the realm of possibility that Melanie Grady represented such a person.

His cell phone rang, startling him, and he reached for it.

He glanced at the screen and immediately answered. "Merry Christmas, Keti."

"Hi. Merry Christmas to you!"

She sounded different, different than she'd sounded for years.

"I have a dog," she told Martin.

"What?"

Keti was notorious for her determination not to live with anything that needed care to survive—not even a houseplant.

"That's great. What kind?" He pictured an expensive breed imported from somewhere exotic. Still, taking care of something else *alive,* something outside herself, had to be a step in the right direction.

"Mmm. Well, he's a mutt, I guess. He was stuck to the screen door last night with porcupine quills. Awful, wasn't it, Marley, buddy?"

"Marley?" Keti must be talking to the dog.

"Yes. For my aunt. She won't mind. I guess. I mean, she wasn't much of a dog person herself.

"Anyhow, he'd been skunked, too, but now we're good friends. Are you at Tiffany's? I'm coming over later, and I wanted to find out the time. I mean, what time she wants us—her note didn't say."

"Probably one o'clock. I told her I'd be there by then. Does this mean you're going to bury the hatchet?"

"What hatchet?" she asked nonchalantly.

"I think you and your employee, my niece, have had words recently."

According to Tiffany, the subject had been the crowded condition of the trailer park. *Why don't you open another one?* Tiffany had asked Keti. *Or help us get one of those build-to-own programs here in Bounty? This place is becoming horrible.*

And Keti had said, *Why is it my problem? There are certainly cheaper places to live than Bounty. You don't have to live here.*

Well, that was Keti.

"She asked me to come for Christmas dinner," Keti said, as if this was answer enough to the hatchet question. "Are you at home?" she asked. "Why aren't you already at Tiffany's. Are you on call?"

"No, I'm at home. I've got something to do here before I drive over, though." A few things. Because he realized that he hadn't expected Keti at this year's celebration. Tiffany had told her uncle *she* didn't expect Keti. For the first time he could remember since childhood, he had no gift planned for Keti Whitechapel. And he kicked himself for that, whether she'd planned to come to Tiffany's or not. "Tell me again how you wound up with a dog."

"I *told* you," she said impatiently. "He was on my back porch and he wouldn't leave, and he was stuck on the screen door."

"And you didn't call animal control?" Martin mused.

She cares about you, Martin. She always has.

The thought made him uncomfortable. If he had shown her love, love that was truly unconditional, couldn't he have brought about the change he'd hoped to see in her?

Well, maybe this dog could do what Martin hadn't been able to accomplish.

It was never your place to change her, Martin.

"I did call the marshal, but everyone was out on a call. Some accident. Anyhow, now Marley and I are friends, and he's my dog. You can meet him today. I guess I'll see you around one," she added, sounding preoccupied.

"Yes."

Keti hadn't bought a single present this year. Ever since her friendship with Martin had fizzled out, there hadn't been anyone she wanted to remember. Or so it had seemed.

But it was different now. There were people in Bounty who probably didn't have money to buy presents for their families, and Keti could have helped them. In fact, she still could.

But first she must make a list. She started with everyone who was likely to be at Tiffany's house.

She felt ashamed, as she realized how easy it would have been to have bought a toy for each of Tiffany's children—and how selfish she'd been not to do so. She could give five hundred dollars to each member of the extended Collins family and never feel the lack herself.

Fortunately, her own house had almost limitless potential as a source of gifts. There were two picture-perfect children's rooms, one equipped with a special "secret" hideaway that overlooked the staircase. And all the child-friendly spaces were packed with toys— the decorator's idea. Keti had never seen the point, but she hadn't cared enough to argue about it. Now, she would wrap up some of these and take them to Tiffany's. Tiffany would know where they'd come from, but the children certainly wouldn't care.

There was no wrapping paper, but Keti found copies of *Architectural Digest* and *Dwell* and tore out the prettier, more colorful pages to use. What should she give Tiffany? And what about that husband of hers, Tim? Tim loved motorcycles. Did she own anything that fit with that? And what about Martin's father?

And what about Martin himself?

For so many years, Martin had wanted her to change, to become a more generous person, and now she was determined to do so. It had taken an extraordinary night to remind her that it is enjoyable to give.

I want to be different. I love the person I am, the person I'm capable of being. Martin didn't matter.

Martin always matters to you, Keti.

She had tried, so many times, to stop herself from loving him. Again and again, she'd failed.

He never thought I was good enough, because I was so stingy.

Now that she was changing, was it possible he could love her? Would he want her? And how would she feel about that? About the fact that she'd had to become someone else in order to be accepted?

Keti didn't like the answer to the last question.

She'd always wanted Martin to love her just as she was.

And because she'd known that he never would, she'd given up their child for adoption.

Stupid, stupid, selfish, selfish.

At 8:00 a.m., Martin called the Hot Springs Motel and asked them to ring Melanie Grady's room.

On the first ring, someone picked up the phone. "Hello?"

"This is Martin Collins, returning your call."

"Ah, thank you. Are you in Bounty?"

"Yes," Martin answered slowly. "What's this about?"

"Is there any chance you could meet me for a coffee or breakfast?"

Martin considered the request. The Bounty ski resort was open. So, there would be *some* place open to eat. "Where?" he asked.

"Well, there's a breakfast room here. I'll treat."

"All right. Can you tell me what this is about?"

"I'd prefer to talk about that in person," the woman replied.

"Right."

"Can you make it by nine?"

He considered all the things that were undone—
and the one gift he still had to produce somehow.
"Make it ten."

Martin hastily packed his truck with gifts he'd
selected for his family and a batch of brownies he'd
made the night before.

For so many years, Keti's gift had been the one
he'd thought about most of all. How could he have
let it go this year? he wondered.

Maybe it was because she'd cried when he'd criti-
cized her over the tin of cookies.

He wasn't obligated to give Keti or *anyone* a
present. But would Keti be receiving presents from
anyone who truly cared about her this Christmas? Let
alone anyone she actually loved?

There had never been a year when he hadn't
wanted to give her a gift.

Why had he just let the thought slip away this
year?

Because he'd been hoping he could let her slip
away, too.

That hadn't happened. Yes, he'd resisted spending
time with her, resisted raising her hopes that they
might someday share any more than they did. But
this year she'd also resisted him. When he'd talked

to her about the clinic, one of their few recent conversations, she'd been especially snotty, making it
abundantly clear that she didn't care all that much
about him or his projects.

*What would you have gotten for her this year,
Martin, if you'd known she was going to be at Tiffany's?*

Could he *make* her a gift? He could certainly make
a card. How much time did he have before his
meeting with Melanie Grady?

Inside, he went to his bedroom with its simple
IKEA bed. In a shoe box in the closet, he kept many
of his old photos.

Photos you never look at anymore, Martin.

What if he made a photo gift of the years they had
known each other?

Why not? He had paper and glue somewhere.

He gathered supplies on the rough wooden table
in the kitchen—the solid rustic table that was the
centerpiece of his home.

He'd had dreams once of Keti sharing this home.
And briefly, she had. What had gone wrong?

His own judgmental streak.

He had always judged Keti, and he knew it and
didn't like it in himself. How could he ever call her
selfish after that one sacrifice she'd made, of her own
child?

Of that child…

Did part of him judge her for not raising her daughter herself?

Who appointed you God, Martin Collins?

Keti's desire to give was suddenly overwhelming, and she went through her closet weeding out everything she didn't absolutely love. She would make it a true Bounty day at the free box.

Marley sniffed his way through the house. When he wanted to go outside, Keti faced the fact that he had no collar and she certainly had no leash. Using a piece of clothesline to serve as both, she took him out into her yard. Marley was *not* going to be allowed to roam and get hit by a car or worse.

Then she scrambled eggs for both of them for breakfast.

Usually, on every other day, she worked out for three hours in her private gym in the back of the Victorian. Today, she'd lift weights, because it would feel good. But maybe after that, instead of using the treadmill, she'd go for a run with Marley.

Like other people, she thought.

Why did the world feel so open today, as if everything good was out there waiting for her?

And what could she give Martin?

She'd think about that on her run with Marley. Maybe she'd make something. Or write a poem. It wouldn't have to be brilliant; it could just include some of the things she felt about him.

Oh, the world was so different—and so beautiful—this Christmas Day.

The woman who met Martin in the lobby of the Hot Springs Motel was no more than twenty-two, Martin decided when he saw her. Probably about five foot six, with wire-rimmed glasses, wearing a Patagonia jacket that looked as though it had seen many backpacking trips. Her reddish-blond hair was shoulder length, her skin freckled.

Martin said, "Melanie Grady?"

"Yes. You're Martin Collins."

"Merry Christmas," Martin said.

"Likewise."

They went into the motel's small glassed-in pool area surrounding the indoor hot springs. A folding table against one wall contained a spread of rolls, coffee, hot water, tea bags and juice.

Martin and his companion filled plates and coffee cups, then went to sit at one of the tables near the pool.

Melanie gazed directly into Martin's face. "Sixteen years ago, you accompanied a woman to the Bounty hospital when she gave birth to a child."

Martin's heart pounded once—hard.

His first thought was that this girl was Keti's child. She didn't look like Keti, but she wouldn't necessarily.

Nor did she look anything like...

He cast that thought aside, but his guard was up—on Keti's behalf. This was Keti's business. It had to do with the adoption. He could reveal nothing without her permission. Her privacy was his foremost concern, and he would protect her. He could tell her what this person wanted, whoever she turned out to be, but he couldn't say what he knew.

He asked instead, "How did you reach that conclusion?"

"Detective work. Some papers that came into her adoptive parents' hands had you listed as the emergency contact for the mother. There was a man with the birth mother at the clinic. It turns out he was a physician, but not *her* physician. So, by the way, you *can* tell me what you know."

In her opinion.

"Her adoptive parents knew these things," Melanie continued. "So I came here to see you."

Martin sat in silence. Silence was safe and would not betray Keti.

Melanie Grady seemed to wait a moment for Martin to speak. Then, realizing that wasn't going to happen, she continued her own story. "The girl who was born here in Bounty is my sister. We're both adopted. But she's my sister, Charlotte. Two years ago, she assisted some motorists in a bad car accident over in Denver and she was exposed to—and contracted—hepatitis B. Now, her liver is failing. She needs a liver transplant. A blood relative would be the ideal donor. A living donor could give part of his or her liver and the donor's liver would grow back, regenerate. It could save Charlotte's life. She's a pretty incredible person."

"What are your parents doing?" Martin asked. *Why aren't they here pursuing this?* Or were they with Charlotte?

"They were killed in the car accident. The same one... I was driving. Charlotte and I were unharmed. I'm her guardian now."

"Good God," Martin said. The guilt... But he couldn't say anything. He couldn't even admit to Melanie Grady that he knew Charlotte's birth mother. Charlotte's mother. As for Charlotte's father...

Thoughtfully, he said, "I'd like a way to contact you. I know they'd like a blood relative as a donor, but I do know other people who would also be willing to do this. I would myself." *Yes. A blood relative would be best.*

"But what I want..."

"I know what you want," Martin interrupted. "I'm sorry. I don't have anything else to say right now but that, myself, I'd be glad to help."

Melanie's eyes grew sharp. "Are you her father?"

Martin gave an internal ironic laugh, and he was

surprised by his own succinct answer, by how swiftly it came. "No."

Her eyes swiftly searched his face. Then, her expression suddenly grim, she reached for the Guatemalan bag she'd slung over the back of her chair and opened it. She picked through the contents and withdrew an envelope. "In the event you do happen to run into her birth mother—or just someone you think might be interested—you might give the person this."

He had taken the envelope before he knew it. Already knowing the answer, he asked, "What is this?"

But he was opening the envelope now, and Melanie Grady did not answer.

He withdrew a photograph of a dark-haired young woman. She bore an uncanny resemblance to his own sister Amy.

Keti was running with Marley, and she had just waved to some skiers hiking to the gondola that would take them up the mountain. They'd called, "Merry Christmas!" and she had responded with the same.

Her cell phone chimed. A simple generic melody. Nothing fancy.

She slowed and Marley looked up at her with a happy dog smile, then sniffed a large rock near the trailhead they'd approached. As he lifted his leg, Keti looked down at the screen. Martin. She answered.

"Keti, I want to see you alone."

"That's new," she responded immediately.

Silence. A silence that seemed a reprimand for her near flirtation.

You're still so aloof, she thought with regret.

"A young woman contacted me last night. She wanted to see me. Keti, she's from—" a breath-like hesitation "—your daughter's adoptive family."

Her dreams of the previous night rushed at her. "She's not my daughter," she whispered, wanting desperately to lean on something, anything.

"Well, you know who I mean. She has hepatitis B and she urgently needs a liver transplant. I didn't tell this kid—her sister, also adopted—anything. That's for you to do, if you want." Then, he told her everything Melanie Grady had told him. His voice sounded strange, emotionless and flat, and yet it was also teeming with emotion.

Keti blinked. "I actually need my own liver." Her daughter...flesh and blood...yet not hers.

Not hers and Martin's. *Oh, God. Oh, God. Why is this happening?*

"Actually," he said, "you can donate part of yours, and it regenerates. The risk to you is low."

"Really?" She considered. "I could do that." She *would* do that. Of course she would. And she could see this person, this child, the walking, talking creature to whom she'd given birth and who was now almost a grown woman.

Who had no parents now.

No parents but…me?

And Martin.

I can never tell him. He'll hate me if he knows the truth.

He asked, "Would you like to call her yourself?"

I'm scared. I'm not her parent, whoever she is. Just a stranger who gave her away. She won't like me.

"The sister," Martin clarified. "Her name is Melanie. Your… They named her Charlotte. Charlotte Anne Grady."

Charlotte.

As in her dream.

"I…" She didn't know what to do, what to say. "Yes, I think. Or, maybe you should—call, I mean. Maybe that would be…"

"Why don't I pick you up? To go to Tiffany's. You can think about it in the meantime."

"Yes. Yes."

Keti had a Christmas wreath on the door when Martin came to pick her up. But maybe the wreath was Tiffany's doing. Keti's disinterest in Christmas had become legendary in Bounty over the years.

Martin's knock was answered by sharp barks. When Keti opened the door, the animal darted out, barked once, and then jumped all over him.

"Marley, you can't do that. Sorry, Martin, he

doesn't have a collar yet. Marley, get down! Is the grocery store open?" As it had been in her dream. "I could get him a collar there."

"Let's find out," he said, crouching to pet the exuberant dog, stroking the one ear that bent forward at the tip. "You deserve a collar," Martin said, admiring Marley's pale blue eyes.

Keti was different. Martin recognized this at once, thinking to himself that she even *looked* somewhat different. Stepping inside, into a foyer crowded with bags full of Christmas presents, Martin glanced toward the arch where mistletoe had hung in other years. None there now.

Keti wore jeans—unusual for her—and a red hooded sweatshirt, and her blond hair looked slept-on and disheveled and soft. On her feet were running shoes that had been splattered with mud.

"You look…casual," he found himself saying.

"Is that a problem?" she snapped.

He bit back a smile. "You are beautiful, always."

Her expression was an appealing mixture of ruefulness, self-deprecation and gratitude.

His heart lurched. "Will you let me buy Marley's collar?"

"I suppose. Should we measure him? I think I have a tape measure somewhere."

The dog wriggled happily as the two of them

crouched on the kitchen floor to determine the size of his neck.

"Want a coffee or anything?" Keti asked.

Martin eyed the gleaming restaurant-quality espresso maker, which probably received little use. "Sure. Thank you."

He stood beside her as she prepared to make him a drink.

"Cappuccino?"

"Thanks."

Marley sat and watched the process with interest.

Martin was thinking of Charlotte.

Of the picture he hadn't told Keti he possessed. Though he would give it to her. And watch her face as she saw how much Charlotte Anne Grady looked like Amy.

"Is Marley housebroken?" Martin asked.

"Well, he hasn't done anything indoors yet. He must have had a home at one point."

When she steamed the milk for Martin's drink, the dog tilted his head sideways.

"You are adorable," Keti told Marley.

"Thank you," Martin replied.

"I've *always* said that you are," she answered.

When she handed him the steaming mug of coffee, Martin spontaneously leaned toward her and kissed her on the lips. The brief touch reminded him, as only Keti could make him remember, everything it was to be a man.

Keti said, "I think I'll be in love with you till I die."

She did not tell him that the one thing she feared, feared above all other things, was a time when he might be taken from her. She did not tell him that the only moments of happiness she'd ever known with a lover had been in his arms.

She remembered that the lesson of her dream was that the true joy in life came from giving.

Though that dream had come before the particular dilemmas of this day.

If she was to help Charlotte as she wanted to do, could she do so without telling Martin the complete truth?

And what if she turned out to be an unsatisfactory donor?

Then she'd have to tell Martin the truth, and damn the consequences.

As if she could ever take the consequences of angering Martin so lightly. Though, could it really make things worse? He had rejected her not once but many times.

Martin felt her withdraw slightly. "What is it?" he asked.

"Oh…nothing. Maybe I'm just tired of my own instincts. I find myself wanting to measure up to your expectations. I've never done it, and I wonder, if I did, I'd simply resent that you'd never loved me as I am."

"I've *always* loved you," Martin replied. "I've just

never believed I could live with you. Peacefully, I mean. We're so different."

"But we did live peacefully for a while, after you came back from Vietnam. Unfortunately, at some point you began to judge who I am."

Martin didn't deny it.

"It was the brothels," he said.

"Well, they've been sold for years, though not because of you."

"I know. You never told me why."

She gave an explanation. For years, she told him, she'd had no difficulty finding good managers, keeping up with health regulations and everything else that was involved in running the businesses. But the profit margin seemed to have shrunk, just as she'd begun to find her managers harder to deal with.

Her mind was only partially on the subject.

Charlotte. She'd dreamed about a girl named Charlotte, and now it turned out that the girl to whom she'd given birth was actually named Charlotte. And Charlotte, the real Charlotte, was dying, Martin had said, or in danger of dying.

"I think," Keti said, "I'd like to call whatever number you have. For Charlotte's sister."

They sat at the table together, and Keti took out her address book to record the information Melanie Grady had given Martin. She set her cordless phone beside her, waiting.

He passed an envelope across the table to her.

Keti knew, could feel, that there was a photograph inside. "Do I want to see this?"

"Definitely," he said, his eyes on her face.

So she took out the snapshot of a girl holding a snowboard and saw immediately what Martin had seen.

She barely looked at the picture, instead stole a glance at him. He watched her, his handsome face unreadable.

She set down the photo and picked up her pen. "The number," she prompted and did not meet his eyes again.

"Keti!" exclaimed Bridget, throwing open the door to Tiffany's trailer.

"Hi, Bridget." Keti tried to focus on the moment, on this Christmas with the Collins family. She and Martin would leave together the next day for California to see her daughter—their daughter—and the young woman's doctors.

Though she and Martin had not discussed what must be as obvious to him as it was to her, that Charlotte was his daughter as much as Keti's.

Keti focused, instead, on the fear.

Charlotte Grady, Melanie had informed her, was extremely ill.

It had been decided that a telephone meeting was not the most appropriate way for Keti to reenter

Charlotte's life. Instead, Martin and Keti would meet Melanie the following day and follow her to California, where Charlotte was hospitalized.

Between themselves, they'd agreed not to discuss this at the Collins family gathering. The last thing Keti wanted to talk about was the experience of giving up her child up for adoption, and Martin had said with some irony that he thought there were other conversations they needed to have first. Which left Keti with the challenge of concealing from the Collinses the life-changing news she'd received earlier in the day.

What she thought about, instead, was the previous time she'd been to Tiffany's house.

She'd brought that tin of cookies, saying to Martin, "I don't really have energy for the Christmas thing." What she'd meant was that she didn't think Tiffany was particularly deserving, and Keti certainly couldn't choose to give presents to some of the Collins family members but not to others.

Well, she was determined to make up for all of that on this occasion.

Martin helped her make two trips from the house with her bags of packages, the numerous gifts wrapped in pieces of magazine. Marley, led to the car and allowed into the backseat, immediately tried to climb up front, standing on the gearshift, wriggling ecstatically.

Keti said, "Marley, you can sit on my lap. Come on."

Martin said, "What's come over you?"

She blinked at him, her blue eyes guileless beneath her mascaraed lashes.

Then, she said, "Okay, it's silly, but last night I had a dream. A bunch of dreams. Like Scrooge. And those dreams changed me in the same way. Though you notice I'm still wearing my Scrooge watch."

He smiled.

Then she told him of the dream that included Charlotte. "And her name was Charlotte," she concluded. "What do you think of all that?"

Martin said, "I think I want to know why you never told me the truth about her."

And there it was.

She sighed. "You would have insisted on marrying me, and I didn't want you to do that—not for that reason. I wanted to be loved for myself. And, yes, I did try to get pregnant and then I made this decision, all these decisions. I was so foolish. I'm sorry. I don't have anything better to say."

Silence.

Then, he started the car.

She said, "I think I should drive myself. This isn't good for me, Martin, this thing that you and I have." She gazed across the street at the lawn decorations in front of her neighbor's home. A Santa Claus, a huge, inflatable snowman. The sky beyond the snow-covered trees and rooftops was blue, and she saw a family in their Sunday best walking together, enjoying Christmas Day.

Martin heard the pain in her voice.

He stopped thinking about Charlotte. But he *couldn't* stop thinking about her. "I knew she was mine."

Keti stared. "You *did?*"

"On some level. Not completely. But how could she have been anyone else's?"

Keti didn't answer this. How, indeed?

She started to open her door, to let herself out.

He reached over and touched her arm. "Keti, I didn't believe I'd be a good parent."

"You?" she said in disbelief. "You think you're good in every way. I'm not buying this."

He still didn't want to talk about the war. He never spoke of it. But now he said, "After you kill people, things are different."

Well, he'd certainly chosen a defense she couldn't argue with, Keti thought. She knew, as well, that there would be no point in asking him to explain why having been a soldier ruled out fatherhood. He wouldn't be able to put it into words. But she believed him. She sighed, sighed at herself, loving this man who could be so holier-than-thou to the rest of the world, then admit this was who he was inside.

"It's no excuse," he said. "It's up to me, Keti. My

shortcomings are my doing." Then, "You didn't want to keep her, either."

"No," she said. What she'd wanted was his love. With that, she *would* have wanted to raise Charlotte herself. Without him, her self-doubt had been too great.

Self-doubt fed by him, by his criticism of her?

His right hand closed over her left, and Marley tried to climb into his lap. Martin gently discouraged this. "Not in the driver's seat, Marley." He said, "I love you, Keti. I have always loved you."

She waited for him to say more, to say *something* that would bring her peace.

"Yes, well," she said at last, indistinctly, removing her hand from his. "As I said, perhaps I should take Marley in my car. I mean, there's no reason to pretend…"

"We're friends, Keti. We've always been friends. We'll always be friends. We're family, in a way, too."

Abruptly, she reached for the door handle.

Again, he reached past her. Her wrist was small and delicate. "Keti, I'm no good at this."

"You're right," she said abruptly. "I've never been good enough, and no one *can* be good enough. Look, why don't you just take these gifts over to Tiffany's. Marley and I can find something else to do today."

"Keti, *no*. I'm the one who's not good enough. Don't you get it?"

"I get that. I just don't *believe* you feel that way.

It's always been about how selfish and materialistic I am and how you have different values."

"Keti, I have too much to make up for. I never will make up for it, but I can't stop trying, and I couldn't risk anything that might not make me a better person."

"Good. Don't risk it."

"Don't go," he said. "Please. I'm going to buy Marley's collar, and I want to spend this day with you. It matters to me to spend today with you."

"Why?"

"Because I love you, which I've just told you."

"Yes, you love me, the way you love your impoverished patients, as if I'm a project. I've always been a project with you, from the first time your parents made you ask me to spend Christmas with you. That's not real love, Martin. It's charity, like that. Giving just to make yourself feel good because you've been generous. Oh, people are grateful sometimes. But no one who simply wants to be loved will be grateful for that."

He heard her and recognized her words for truth.

He also knew that he had loved Keti differently, and that he was afraid of that kind of love, the kind that needed a particular person.

He said, "Keti, I want to spend Christmas with *you*. In the selfish way you want me to feel."

Chapter 12

At Tiffany's, later that day

Tiffany looked at the snow leopard puppet Crazy Horse had just unwrapped. She squinted at Keti. "Is that the one from upstairs at your house?"

Keti blushed and cursed Tiffany's bad manners. The snow leopard *looked* new, and it had lost fifty dollars when the interior decorator had purchased it for Keti's house. "Yes, as a matter of fact," she said. "I didn't know what I was doing for Christmas until this morning, strange as that sounds."

Hands closed on her shoulders, and she looked up

from the couch where she was sitting beside Crazy Horse. The hands were Martin's, and spontaneously he bent over, embracing her tightly, his head near hers. "And I, for one, am glad she decided to do this."

Marley lay on the floor near one of the trailer's heater vents. He'd been fed Christmas cookies by Tiffany's oldest daughter, and he'd devoured the Christmas gifts that Martin and Keti had bought for him at the store—all that were edible. He wore his new red leather collar, and his head rested on a stuffed squeaky toy, a dog that looked a bit like him.

"She never got religion, but at least she got a dog," Martin's brother George had quipped as he greeted Keti and Marley.

"It's lucky you had so many things around your house that you never use," Tiffany pointed out.

"Yes," Keti agreed, ignoring the barb.

"What did she give you?" Tiffany asked Martin.

"I haven't given him his present yet," Keti answered, knowing she didn't want to give it to him in front of the rest of his family—and particularly not in the presence of Tiffany. Tiffany was demonstrating, Keti couldn't help but think, exactly how much she valued her job as property manager of Keti's Victorian. Keti also couldn't help thinking, *I should fire her.*

The notion was at odds with every new resolution she'd made that morning.

Disappointment flowed through her at the possibility that life really *hadn't* changed, that even the way she looked at it hadn't shifted all that much.

But I won't fire Tiffany, she thought.

And she probably never would have, even though Tiffany had been rude and cruel.

Keti wished she had a real present for Martin—that she'd bought her gifts in advance, rather than assembling them from what she'd had on hand. She recollected her trip to the free box earlier that morning and the eager residents waiting there, who were so thrilled as she'd unloaded her car.

She wished she felt the elation now that she'd felt at that moment. She wished the feeling had lasted.

Martin knelt behind the couch. Head near hers, he said, "I haven't given you your gift, either."

"Want to come back to the house later?" she asked.

"I do."

They brewed cider on her stove and took it upstairs to her bedroom. Marley looked accusingly at Martin when he stretched out on Keti's bed. Then, the dog jumped up beside him—between Martin and Keti.

"I don't think he approves of me," Martin remarked. "Maybe he's holding the collar against me."

Keti made no move either to shift or reprimand the

dog. Instead, she put a small gift wrapped package in front of Martin. "It's dumb," she said. "And it really didn't cost anything."

He placed his package for her on the bed beside Keti. "Mine was last-minute, too."

"You first," Keti said.

She'd made him a wallet, out of a page from a calendar of Ancient Forests and cellophane tape. It had turned out nicely, and she knew from experience that such wallets—she'd made them for herself in the distant past—could hold up quite well.

"Thank you. I love it," he said and kissed her.

Following Martin's lead, Marley kissed her face, too, but then he moved toward the foot of the big bed, turned around in a circle twice and lay down.

Keti unwrapped her package. It was a small handmade book. On the front page was a photograph of Martin and Keti on either side of a snowman. She turned the pages and the pictures took her through all the years she'd known Martin. Childhood, adolescence, the Collins house, Martin after he returned from Vietnam, the two of them as adults in Bounty.

The most recent photo had been taken two years before, at Tiffany's Christmas celebration.

"Thank you," she said. "This is a wonderful present." *It looks like you care,* she was thinking.

Or why would he have had all these photos?

On the other hand, he'd just given them to her.

"Did you give me all your photos?" she asked.

"Oh, I have some favorites tucked away."

After a moment, she said, "You'll never forgive me, will you? For not telling you."

"There's nothing to forgive. I didn't make it easy for you. I didn't…take care of you as I should have, Keti. I'm sorry. Do you understand and believe what I said? That I didn't feel I'd be a good father?"

She supposed that in some way she did believe.

"And do you forgive *me?*" he asked.

She nodded. She nodded because there was no point in *not* forgiving him. She also nodded because she believed that he was saying that his reasons for rejecting her had more to do with himself than with her own shortcomings.

They set their gifts on the bedside table, and Martin reached for her.

Keti said suddenly, "Do you think it will work?"

"The liver transplant?"

"Yes."

"I don't know," he admitted.

How could she suddenly get back her daughter and possibly lose her, as well?

Maybe it would be better actually not to meet her. She told Martin this.

"Always err on the side of love, Keti."

She gave a wry laugh. "Do you?"

"No." He paused. "But I still know it's the right way to be."

"Will you tell her," Keti asked, "that you're her father?"

"I'd like to. I think," he added softly.

"You're unsure?"

"My doubts about myself haven't evaporated. But I want to meet her. And I know that I'll want her to know. She won't understand," he said. "She probably won't understand any of this."

"No. She's too young." *And how could she, when I barely understand?*

The subject of money had not raised its head this Christmas, and Keti didn't want to address it.

She'd given thought over the years to Mrs. Collins's suggestion that letting a woman support him would gall Martin. Perhaps the fact that she, Keti, was so much wealthier than he was had the same effect. She said, "I've never stopped being in love with you."

"I think that's safer for you," he answered.

"Safer than what?"

"Than loving, well, any of a host of different people."

There was some truth to what he said. "Safe, maybe," she agreed. "But not always comfortable."

Because Martin wasn't a man who talked about his feelings. Other people's feelings, sometimes. But not his. And he appeared, often, to believe that Keti should know his feelings for her—whatever they were—without his telling her. His actions, he thought, should demonstrate to her how he felt about her.

But his actions were ambiguous sometimes. And then, there was the fact that sometimes he wanted his actions to *say* something, and that he chose them for what he thought he was saying—which wasn't necessarily what he felt. And what he'd decided to say was often what he'd decided was good for everyone involved, based on some obscure reasoning that made sense only to him.

Martin said, "This is such a comfortable bed."

"It is," she agreed. "Sometime you'll have to try out the bathtub."

"How big a hot water heater do you need to be able to fill that thing?"

"Large," she said with a small smile.

"You know, it would have been good for my ego years ago," he said, "if there'd been something I could have given you that you couldn't give yourself."

Just as his mother had said.

Interesting.

"There has always been plenty!" Keti exclaimed. "You know that perfectly well."

"I mean, that you're a little too good at taking care of yourself."

"Well, it's not as though, if I hadn't been, you would have wanted to take care of me."

"Keti, I always want to take care of you. But there's not much left for me to do."

"This," she said, angry all at once. Here they were, two people leaving middle age, familiar with each other's bodies, with every freckle, with every imperfection. And Martin was coming out with this nonsense.

But he smiled into her face with the expression of peaceful reverence that she always associated with him. As if, for him, she embodied all women.

As for her, he embodied all good men.

It was the best Christmas Keti could remember.

They watched *Miracle on 34th Street* on DVD on the big-screen television in the upstairs den, took a bath together and got back into bed again.

Nonetheless, Keti wanted to ask, *So what happens now? What happens tomorrow? Will you be my lover again? Will we sleep in each other's arms for a few nights and then lose each other once more?*

And where would Charlotte fit into all of this?

She sighed involuntarily.

Martin did not ask the reason for the sigh. Instead, he drew her close to him, until her head lay against his chest, over the strong, steady beat of his heart.

Safe, Keti thought. *I'm safe.*

Chapter 13

One year into the future

It was a Christmas to begin new traditions. This was Keti's first Christmas as Mrs. Martin Collins.

And it was Martin's first Christmas married to one of the richest women in the country.

It was the first Christmas that they lived together in *their* new house, the rebuilt Old House—including its natural hot spring, the first place Keti and Martin had so much as kissed and the place they had found each other.

Perhaps most of all, it was Keti and Martin's first

Christmas with their daughter, Charlotte, and Charlotte's sister, Melanie.

Keti awoke beside Martin in the master bedroom of the Old House. The house was full, not only with Charlotte and Melanie and Melanie's boyfriend, but also with the entire Collins family. Martin had told his family that he hoped *this* would be the house where they would always gather in Christmases to come.

The first half year of marriage had not been entirely easy. Keti had learned that becoming generous with all she had was not a cure-all for Martin's concerns about her income—or for the doubts he had about himself, the legacy of a long-ago war, almost never expressed in words. Only to her, who knew him best, were these doubts apparent.

Yet Keti feared the issues of wealth and want would always separate them in some way. She had become so extraordinarily good at making money and Martin would never be comfortable taking it from her—a good quality, actually. He worked and worked hard and would no doubt be a hard worker all his life. But he possessed an almost invisible chip on his shoulder when it came to financial questions. And they had found no comfortable way around the issue.

When it came to gifts for his family, he had trouble accepting *her* money as *their* money. There had been no prenuptial agreement. Keti trusted Martin. It was as simple as that. She'd known him for decades and knew that anger would not change his morals, would not allow him to justify wrongs.

Charlotte had made a remarkable recovery after her liver transplant, and Keti had healed in record time. And now she had the unexpected gift of knowing her seventeen-year-old daughter—seventeen today.

Now Charlotte was living in Bounty with Keti and Martin and finishing high school there. Melanie and her boyfriend had moved to Bounty, as well, where they worked in the ski industry in the winter and one of Bounty's better restaurants in the summer.

There were sacrifices Keti made now that were not as comfortable as simple philanthropy. She'd always loved having a maid, but Martin disliked having household servants. He wouldn't have vetoed a maid, and he certainly shared the housework.

In any event, it was no mean feat for two people who'd been single for more than fifty years to suddenly find themselves with a shared home and a shared life.

Keti hoped very much that Martin would like his main gift this year. It was an echo of what his parents had always done for each other at Christmas.

In this case, she'd given an anonymous gift of a thousand dollars to an impoverished family in Bounty.

Since there was no receipt, she'd simply written a note to Martin to say what she'd done. This was to be her gift to him, to help someone else, just as his parents had done for each other every Christmas.

She'd given away other money, as well, and she'd asked Martin to help her make decisions, although he still wasn't comfortable with the idea of her money being their money.

"Keti." Sleepily, he reached for her, pulling her closer to him, and she felt the warmth of his skin and acknowledged the absolute trust she felt for him.

"Merry Christmas," she said.

"Merry Christmas to you."

Keti went into her "instantly awake" mode, getting up, showering, dressing and stepping out into the kitchen, all in record time.

Charlotte emerged from her room sleepily.

Charlotte was a tall girl, whose resemblance to Martin's sister Amy remained astonishing.

"Hi, Keti," Charlotte said. She had never called her Mom, and Keti accepted this. In her own mind, she didn't deserve to be treated as a mother. She'd had so little to do with raising Charlotte. It was a gift to know her daughter now and to see the things they had in common.

Charlotte said she'd never had the warmest relationship with her adoptive parents. She'd always felt her differentness. It was with Melanie that she was closest. The adopted sisters were best friends and had been allies growing up, living under rules that had sometimes seemed too inflexible to them.

"Good morning, Charlotte," Keti greeted her. "Happy birthday!" She embraced her daughter and kissed her cheek. "What do you say we have a big breakfast?"

Then a small figure emerged from the carpeted hallway.

"Tim!" Keti cried.

Tiffany's youngest son walked toward her sleepily and lifted up his arms in a universal gesture that needed no translation.

Keti picked him up. Tiffany had taken him to France that summer, and the change since then in both mother and child was dramatic. Now Tiffany was taking French at the community college in the next town. As part of her Christmas gift to Tiffany, Keti planned to offer her a job at the mine office, with a chance to expand her responsibilities and oversee projects—including the reclamation of a small South African mine. Tiffany had been transformed by her new desire to see more of the world, and her husband's work actually allowed her some freedom to be away from home. He could and often did have the children with him at his recently expanded shop, which now sold snowmobiles in addition to motorcycles.

Little Tim, Tiny Tim, had benefitted from his treatment by a French specialist. The physician there had shown Tiffany new ways to help her son with his learning, and Tiffany had shared these methods with the rest of the family.

Tim's development seemed to become more "normal" every day. He loved to be read to, for example. Taking the idea from a parenting book she'd found at the library, Keti had printed the names of everyday household items on cards and taped the cards to various things. Yesterday, Charlotte had even found a way to tape a card that read Dog onto Marley's collar.

Keti kissed the little boy and said, "Merry Christmas. Did you look under the tree to see if Santa came?"

Tim shook his head.

"Let's go look!" Charlotte suggested.

Soon, others came into the kitchen, and Keti heard more voices in the living room as she took eggs from the refrigerator and a bag of pancake mix from the cupboard. Crazy Horse, Chaparral and Athena had *not* forgotten to check and see if Santa Claus had come.

Bridget's younger daughter, Samantha, then came into the kitchen with the newest member of the Collins clan, Cameron, who was three weeks old.

Keti greeted her niece and great-nephew joyfully. She couldn't believe there'd ever been a time when she'd turned away from the delight of an infant. Of course, after she'd given up Charlotte, her feelings had shut down temporarily. But truly, underneath, where she discussed it with *no one,* she had never ceased feeling the void left by Charlotte.

"Can you take him for a minute?" Samantha asked.

"Twist my arm," said Keti, carefully taking the infant from his mother, marveling at his tiny fingernails, at his perfect features. "Actually, if you want to take time for a shower, I can watch him while you do."

"Thanks be," Samantha answered and hurried from the room.

Martin came in to find Keti at the kitchen table, drinking coffee and gazing in wonder at Cameron.

Smiling, he walked over, pushed back the blond hair now streaked with silver, and kissed his wife. "You glow when you hold that baby."

"Who wouldn't?" Then ruefully, she answered her own question silently. *Me, a year ago.* "I wish they didn't live so far away." Samantha, her husband and son had driven to Bounty from Las Vegas.

"You're spoiled," Martin told her. "What if they lived in Massachusetts?"

"Oh, I know." Keti wanted to discuss something with Martin, but she felt foolish even bringing it up. She was less than a decade away from becoming a senior citizen. "Would it be silly…" She stopped herself. Martin *wouldn't* tell her that she was silly. "I've been thinking of taking some nursing courses. I could do some online and some at the community college. Is this entirely pointless at my age?"

"It's a wonderful idea," he responded. "What's wrong with your age?"

"Well, I'm fifty-six, Martin."

"And?"

She rolled her eyes.

Cameron shifted and blew some bubbles.

"Oh, I love it when you blow bubbles," Keti told him.

Cameron's eyes flickered open and with a toothless mouth he yawned.

"I think your care would be a gift to any patient," Martin said. "And good grief, Keti, you're in better shape than many women half your age. Besides, you've had some difficult life experiences that make you…insightful and compassionate."

"You're hilarious," Keti scoffed.

"Nonsense. I'll never forget the birth at the brothel. You were so kind to that prostitute, the Somalian woman. You wouldn't let anyone hurt her feelings."

Keti didn't answer. Since then Fatima had moved to Las Vegas, where she now had a career as a dancer. She'd written to Keti that Sammar and her daughter were doing well. Sammar had gotten out of the life eventually, and Fatima made enough money to support the three of them.

Marlene's brothels closed after her death. Keti tried to find all the girls employment either in the mine offices or at the ski resort. However, most of them chose to seek the same work elsewhere because of the money. When Martin realized this, he was chagrined, but Keti wasn't surprised.

She'd been amused to see him rack his brain trying to think of some form of employment that would pay the women as well as being legal brothel prostitutes did. But the work available to them, even to those who had university degrees, could never compare in terms of earnings.

"I've enjoyed those times when I've been there to help with births," Keti admitted. "And I remember when you encouraged me to become a maternity nurse or even a midwife." Years ago, now. She gazed down into Cameron's face. "I don't feel brave enough for midwifery. I don't think I want the whole responsibility to rest on my shoulders."

"Well, it never does, no matter who you are."

"You mean, physicians aren't God?" she teased him.

He ran his tongue along the inside of his mouth. "I'm afraid that's exactly what I mean. I don't suppose I could have a turn with my great-nephew."

"I've only had him for five minutes," she complained, and then they both laughed.

Martin said, "I love you, Keti."

"Good. Why don't you mix the pancake batter?"

"*Then,* I get Cameron."

"Are you two squabbling over my son again?" asked Samantha's husband, Mac, strolling into the kitchen. "Keti, you're wanted in the living room to referee. The Cartoon Network team and the Football Watchers are in conflict."

"There shouldn't be any games on yet," Keti said.

"Pregame prognostications?" Mac said. "Don't ask me. Basketball's my thing."

Martin grinned triumphantly and reached out for Cameron.

At noon, Keti and Tiffany went for a walk alone, just the two of them, and Keti talked to her niece about the possibility of a more responsible position, with opportunities for travel. She watched Tiffany consider.

Tiffany said, "Don't you also have mining concerns in Zaire?"

"The country is called the Democratic Republic of Congo now," Keti replied with a smile, guessing where Tiffany's question was directed.

"And that used to be the Belgian Congo, right?"

Keti just smiled again.

"Do they speak French there?"

"Indeed," Keti said. "Other languages, too, but certainly, French is useful, and I've often wished mine were better. Before you got a job over there, though—if you want to work in the mining industry, that is—I'd want you to learn a bit more about mining, as well as improving your French."

"I can take mining geology classes," Tiffany said. "They have a big mining technologies department at the community college."

"And you could learn on the job, as well," Keti noted. "Now that I'm thinking of going back to school myself, it's important for me to have some highly qualified assistants."

Tiffany's eyes rounded. A mix of expressions passed over her face in rapid succession. "Am I..."

"What?"

"I'm not sure I'm smart enough, Keti."

"Tiffany, you're talking to a woman who has made a fortune with only a high school education. Let's not hear any more nonsense about you not being smart enough."

"I have terrible English skills," Tiffany pointed out. "And I'm having an awful time with French. It takes forever for all the parts of speech to make sense to me. Though it makes more sense than English, I have to admit."

"You're not the first person to make that observation," Keti replied. "And your math grades have always been good, haven't they?"

"Yes, but everyone says that calculus is harder than trigonometry. And I'm so *old* to be starting a new career."

Keti put an arm around the younger woman's shoulders. "Thirty-one? If you don't have the courage at thirty-one, how am I supposed to find it at fifty-six?"

Tiffany cast her an anxious look, then blurted out, "I haven't always been fair to you, Keti. I thought I knew you, but I really didn't."

"Don't feel bad," Keti said. *I didn't really know me, either.*

Charlotte's reaction to Keti's announcement that afternoon that she planned to start nursing school, was different from Tiffany's. She looked inexplicably depressed.

"What is it?" Keti asked. She and her daughter sat alone in the kitchen with Cameron, who was sleeping in his infant chair between them while his parents enjoyed a couple hours of cross-country skiing.

"It's just...I've thought I wanted to be a nurse. And if you waited, we could take classes together. But I have to finish high school first."

Keti thought about this. *I don't have time to wait. I have so little time.* She said, "This is your senior year. Do you think the school could make arrangements for you to travel to the community college with me and take some classes there? I'm sure we could do some introductory courses together. Also, I'll probably have to fulfill some additional requirements, since I wasn't as good a student as you are."

"But I've lost time because of illness. Still…do you think maybe they'd let me?"

"I think they might. We'll just have to find out." Her heart swelled with happiness. "And I'm so glad you *want* to take some classes with me. Most seventeen-year-old girls don't *want* their mother around."

Charlotte's look was old beyond her years. "Well, most seventeen-year-old girls have always had their mother around."

"I'm sorry you and your adoptive mother didn't get along better," Keti said truthfully. She'd believed she was putting her daughter into a situation where she would be loved and in which she would thrive. And both had been the case, to some degree. But Charlotte had emerged from that childhood, after her adoptive parents' sudden deaths, shy and with curiously low self-esteem. And Keti couldn't help wondering if their sternness and overprotectiveness had brought about this effect.

Now, Charlotte launched into the subject again. "I know I'm supposed to feel grateful that anyone adopted me…"

"No," Keti hastened to interject.

"But there were times when they made me feel as if I could never be good enough. I can't explain it, and I know it had to do with their religious values. They just seemed terrified that I might someday 'fall into sin,' as if it was my human nature to be bad. And maybe it is."

"Never say that," Keti jumped in. "Never *believe* it, Charlotte. It's no one's nature. People *aren't* good or bad—they simply do good or bad things. And believe me, it's easier for some people to be good than for others. I don't know why this is, but I absolutely believe it. Some people just love other people. Martin is like this. He works hard, but he gets such a rush from being with other people, from helping them. I never understood that clearly until I married him. And I'm so *thankful* to be married to a person like that, because his enthusiasm is contagious. He makes me love people far more than I would on my own."

"He's pretty great," Charlotte agreed. "Maybe it will rub off on me—or come out in my genes. I wish I looked more like either of you. I'd be prettier."

"You look like both of us, Charlotte. And you're much more beautiful than you realize." Charlotte's curly hair fell around her face from a center part. There was something Madonna-like in her looks, which was echoed in her unusually mature disposition.

"I'm so tall," Charlotte complained.

"A million times, *I've* wished to be tall like you. You could be a model, you hold yourself so well."

Charlotte shook her head. "I don't want to be. Oh, no."

Cameron was screwing up his face, preparing to howl.

Keti removed him from his seat and held him against her shoulder, supporting his head. "Are you wet, little guy?"

"Bet on it," Charlotte said.

Together, they went into the room Samantha and Mac were using to change the baby, who complained vigorously throughout the procedure.

Keti was happy. She couldn't remember feeling this way at Christmas ever before. Not in the same way.

Yes, it had pleased her when Martin had given her special gifts.

And, yes, she'd also been content, in some way, knowing that she had a place with the Collins family. But this year everything was different.

Martin entered the guest room. He carried an envelope in his hand, an envelope Keti recognized.

He said, "I recognize the writing of my beloved wife on this envelope. May I open it now?"

"Yes," said Keti. "It's your main present."

"I'm going to get this guy to drink out of a bottle," Charlotte said. "I don't think it's fair for Samantha to have to pump, pump, pump, and for Cameron to turn his nose up at the result." She carried the infant from the room.

Martin slit the envelope and withdrew the hand-made card. Keti had made many cards this year, using a block-printing method that Melanie had explained to her. The image was of an infant in a manger with a star shining overhead.

Martin opened the card and read.

Keti saw him swallow and blink.

He stepped forward and embraced her, then abruptly sank down on the edge of the bed.

"What is it?" Keti asked.

He shook his head without speaking.

"Are you all right?"

"Yes. Yes. Of course." But he appeared preoccupied.

"Would you have rather had something else?" she asked. "Your parents always did this, and I thought you liked the tradition."

"Keti, it's the best present you've ever given me."

That was all right, then. So why did he look so strange?

"I should have consulted you." She tried again to get at the reason for his reaction, which she still could not read.

"I never seem to give you much help with that," he said.

"With what?"

"I'm never eager to talk about money with you, or make financial decisions with you—no matter how often you try."

Keti didn't acknowledge how hurt she often was by the behavior he described. Instead, she said, "I've wondered if I set up a medical foundation, and you directed it…"

He shook his head again. "That would be even worse, Keti. Then I'd feel as if my employment was dependent upon you."

"Surely you don't want me to, well, donate my wealth, all of it? Look what we've been able to do with the clinic." The low-income clinic, for which he'd sought a donation more than a year earlier. Now Keti was its main benefactor. "And I would, if you would help me decide what to do with the money."

"No. I think it's a good idea for your money to generate money. You've found so many good things to assist with, so many valuable contributions to make." He changed the subject. "Do you remember when we were kids and you beat me at ice-skating? When we raced? It was when you chipped your tooth."

She grinned. "As I recall, I tricked you, Martin. You wanted to make sure I was all right, and I got up and raced to the finish."

"I didn't see it that way," he told her. "To my way

of thinking, you won, fair and square. You were a faster skater. As you're better at making money than I've ever been."

"You're good with money," she exclaimed. "What nonsense. You don't run through it, at any rate."

"Well, I forgive plenty of debts and I'm not as hard-nosed as perhaps I should be with patients who don't pay."

"You're not going to hell for that," she said, though she knew that some of Martin's nonpaying patients certainly had the wherewithal to pay. They blew their money on other things, and she'd seen them doing it. A little smile teased the corners of her mouth. "I could take over bill collection."

He laughed. He neither agreed to this suggestion nor rejected it. Instead, he said, "I just can't feel right helping you spend the money you've earned. I don't know what to do about that. Also, I know this house is a lot of work for you and that you're used to having help. I think you should have it."

"Maybe you can think of someone who needs the work," Keti suggested, jumping at the notion of a maid. "And I would appreciate it, especially if I'm going to be taking classes in addition to my other responsibilities."

"I'll think of someone," he said slowly. "And directing the clinic is plenty of authority for me, where your philanthropic projects are concerned. In fact, it's all I can do, in addition to my practice. I just…I wish I knew a way to be more gracious with you on this subject."

And I wish, she thought, *that I could somehow let go of the part of me that still makes life uncomfortable for you.*

But she'd been so relieved when he'd spoken of the good things she was doing with her wealth, relieved that she didn't have to relinquish her financial security.

She knew that she should be willing to live without such a huge cushion. And still she knew that, despite her marriage to Martin, she wasn't quite prepared to do so.

Chapter 14

The next Christmas they kept

Fifty-seven. Keti was fifty-seven years old and a licensed practical nurse. She'd completed her training in record time, and Charlotte would complete hers the coming spring. They both planned to continue their studies and become registered nurses, but in the meantime Keti was already working part-time in Martin's office.

The shared work environment brought a new closeness to their relationship. Though she devoted little time to regret, Keti often wished that she'd begun her training—and her work with Martin—earlier.

She also worked one day each week in the emergency room at the Bounty hospital. It was an exciting new life. She'd never imagined she would so enjoy nursing as a career.

On Christmas Eve she was scheduled to work the graveyard shift at the hospital. Martin promised to come in and visit her on her break, which eased the fact that she'd miss part of the family celebration.

At around 11:00 p.m., a mother came in with a boy who'd broken his arm—falling from a ladder, they both said.

But that wasn't it, Keti knew and the doctor knew, and a report would need to be made to social services. Keti had already encountered the family through the low-income clinic, and she was fairly certain that the mother's boyfriend was responsible for the boy's injuries. She wanted to speak to the mother, whose name was Rhonda, to say, *Why don't you at least tell the truth about what happened?*

She tried to remember the words Mrs. Collins had used to her years before, when she was in a difficult situation and considering going to live with Aunt Marlene.

The poverty in which she'd been raised had deeply affected her. Keti had been required to take some psychology courses as part of her training, and they'd prompted her to have some counseling. She'd suffered as a child, and that had made her yearn for money and security. She understood all this intellectually, but somehow she felt incapable of changing.

If only she could help this one woman leave the violent situation in which she lived. Keti gave Rhonda's son, Darwin, some stickers while they waited for him to have his arm seen to. She looked into Rhonda's eyes and silently tried to convey the message: *Please, let me help. Let someone, anyone, help.*

Well, social services was going to intervene on this one in any case, once they saw the report from the emergency room.

She asked gently, "How do you like Miss Yolanda?" The question was addressed to both of them. Miss Yolanda was Darwin's kindergarten teacher.

"I like her," Darwin said.

Rhonda nodded like someone accustomed to saying nothing. Keti suspected she'd been the boyfriend's target, as well.

She bit her lip and said, "Rhonda, we're all on your side here. You know that."

"Reporting me to social services," Rhonda said coolly, "isn't my idea of someone being on my side."

Keti was careful. There was only so much she could say in front of Darwin. And no one had yet *told* Rhonda that there would be a report to social services. She'd guessed about that.

Keti said nothing. It was her responsibility, the

hospital's responsibility, the community's responsibility, to protect this child.

"You don't have a clue how people like us live," Rhonda said tightly, apparently not as unused to talking as Keti had assumed. "You can afford attorneys, anything you want, let alone food."

"Do you need an attorney?" Keti asked.

Rhonda lowered her eyes. "I was just saying."

Keti knew, especially from her experiences owning brothels, that a batterer might threaten to get custody of his victim's children. She wanted to assure Rhonda that this wouldn't happen. At the same time, she knew the truth of what the other woman had said. Wasn't that the reason she'd clung so tenaciously to her own wealth for all these years? To avoid such vulnerability. Perhaps she could find a way to help this woman become safer, more independent. Might she even be a person to help Keti out in her home?

She wished Martin could be here to hear all this. But Martin knew as well as anyone the perils of poverty. And he'd become more comfortable with the whole issue of her wealth over the past year. He would not live on more money than he earned, but he expressed no disapproval at her spending what she liked on what she liked. Fortunately, their goals and desires were usually consistent, so why should he object?

It was 11:30 p.m. when a call came in for the ambulance. An eighty-three-year-old man had felt woozy, then collapsed as he was getting ready for bed. In shock, Keti heard her own address over the radio. "That's Martin's father," she said to the emergency room doctor.

While they were preparing for Mr. Collins's arrival, the police brought in a teenage boy with a serious stab wound. Keti assisted the emergency room physician immediately, while a specialist was paged. Part of the teenager's bowel had been severed, so the first task was simply to save his life.

Mr. Collins was brought to the hospital with Martin, who had ridden along in the ambulance. But the older man had died en route of a massive stroke.

Keti embraced her husband and looked down on the lifeless face of her father-in-law, a man who had been so kind to her for so many years. There was such a difference in a body between life and death; such a change when the soul and spirit were no longer there.

Martin's eyes were filled with tears, but he said calmly, "He had such a good life."

Gradually, he paid attention to the activity elsewhere in the emergency room, and then he heard about the boy who'd just been brought in. "He's in Johanna's class." Johanna was his brother Paul's daughter. "They've dated."

"Recently?" asked Keti.

"Yes."

Martin found out from the police what he could

about the knife fight. Then, he went into the waiting room to meet his family, who had just arrived from Keti's house.

And at the same moment, the emergency room became extremely busy.

It occurred to Keti, as she worked, that she'd believed for so long that money could protect her from most catastrophes. But, in fact, money only gave the illusion of safety. Charlotte, for example, could have been killed in a motor vehicle accident, as her adoptive parents had been.

Keti hadn't understood the fear of losing some-one—other than Martin—before she'd come to know her daughter.

When she returned home Christmas morning, she expected to find everyone in bed.

Martin was outside, however, at the hot springs, where he and Keti had first made love when he re-turned from Vietnam. Keti was surprised to find him there, sitting alone, gazing at the sky.

"I'm sorry," she said.

"No. It's nothing to mourn. The way my mother died—and how young she was—that was different. But to live eighty-three years and then die quickly of a stroke, rather than to fade slowly... In a way, I'm happy for him. He'll still be with me."

Keti slipped out of her clothes and lowered herself into the steaming pool. "I never thought we'd own this," she said. The owner of the land where the Old House sat had never built or rebuilt there. He'd just held on to the property. It had been some of the most expensive undeveloped land in the county.

Martin didn't reply. He had once thought of the hot springs as a sort of public treasure, even though it had been on privately owned land. But now it was clearly part of their home.

Why do you have to possess everything, Keti? he still wondered.

Then he let it go. Keti was not a selfish person.

"You'll miss him," Keti said.

But Martin was already reaching for her, ready to reaffirm life, their life together.

Four years later

Charlotte was home for Christmas with her husband, Jonah. She was five months pregnant, and Keti planned to attend the birth. In the intervening years, she had become a certified nurse-midwife. She had privileges at the Bounty hospital and an office at the low-income clinic. That Christmas, she had five clients who were expecting, none of them due sooner than three months from now.

The house was full, as usual, for the holidays.

On Christmas Eve, Charlotte and Keti sat near the hearth in the living room with Paul's daughter

Johanna. Johanna was reading *Women's Wear Daily.*
She had expensive tastes and a strong appreciation
for money. Keti saw her younger self in Johanna, but
she couldn't remember ever being as ruthlessly am-
bitious as her niece was.

Johanna, who was five foot nine with straight
black hair halfway down her back, had worked as a
model while at the university in Las Vegas. She'd
traveled widely and already had appeared in all of the
major women's magazines.

Johanna was investing her money in more than
clothes. She wanted to open her own modeling agency,
but not in Nevada. In New York. Keti couldn't sit in
judgment of her, and yet it was oddly painful to watch
someone else close to her make decisions that were in
some ways similar to ones she had made in her time.

But Johanna's worst decision, in Keti's opinion,
was her engagement to her current boyfriend, a finan-
cier who was a jerk. Keti suspected that Johanna was
marrying him for his wealth, and she wanted to help
Johanna understand that she would pay for that
choice in the end. But she would speak of none of it
in front of Charlotte.

Keti waited until her daughter finally announced
she was exhausted and headed for the bedroom to
join her husband. Then Keti and Johanna were left
alone by the fire.

Keti glanced toward the hall. Paul and his wife had

turned in hours before. They always rose at 6:00 a.m. to run, rain or shine.

Marley, old now but still healthy, made his way into the living room and lay down near Keti.

She said, "So, you're sure about Grant?"

Johanna blinked, then smiled suddenly. "I think you might be the one person in the family who can understand how sure I am."

Keti didn't know whether or not to be pleased by the statement. "Why?"

"Well, you know how it is to appreciate money. Building wealth. That's what Grant does. I share his goals and he supports mine."

Keti nodded slowly. If that was true, who was she to offer an opinion? "And he's nice to you."

"To be perfectly honest, I doubt he'll be faithful. However, he'll be *married* to me."

Keti felt terror, now, lest Paul should somehow overhear his daughter's confession. What was it that had led Johanna to make such a compromise?

But Keti knew.

The desire for money.

How did one come to love money so much? So much that she would do anything for it. Even marry for it; marry someone who would be unfaithful.

"Does he love you?" Keti asked, hesitantly.

"He *wants* me. And I want him. He wants me as a trophy, a beautiful wife. I want him for his wealth."

Keti's horror grew. She whispered, "Johanna, whatever you know or believe about my need for security—for money—believe me that I would never have married for it." It astonished her to hear her own words. Yet they were true.

The girl shrugged, though she looked hurt. "Anyhow, I'm doing it."

Keti didn't reply. What could she say? She must tell Martin of this conversation—they kept no secrets from each other. Would he tell his brother? She was torn. Johanna's blithe acceptance of her intended's future infidelity, her admission that she was marrying without love, were personal revelations. Keti didn't judge Johanna, but she was immeasurably saddened by what she had just been told.

Fidelity, long years together, children, *love*... None of these appeared to matter to Johanna. She sounded as if she'd been programmed. And Keti couldn't believe that her niece was really like that inside.

Despite the evidence to the contrary.

Johanna was twenty years old, her values already developed in one particular direction. Torn, undecided, Keti said tentatively, "I think you're making a mistake. And I don't think I can keep this from Martin, Jo. And he may not be able to keep it from your father."

Johanna shrugged. "Well, if my dad chooses to be unhappy about it, that's his business."

God, Keti thought.

"I don't have secrets from Martin," Keti repeated. "Has Grant *said* he's going to fool around?"

"Well, the fact is, he already does. But I intend to *keep* him, when all is said and done."

"But what about diseases, Johanna? You could end up with AIDS."

"I don't think Grant will let that happen."

Right, Keti thought.

She considered her own life with Martin, the fact that neither of them would consider sharing the physical expression of their love with anyone outside their marriage. And there was so much more to their relationship—their deep love, which was based on long knowledge of each other, shared experiences, friendship. Didn't Johanna want that kind of life? She certainly could have it. She could have a *wonderful* husband and children she would treasure.

Keti didn't know what else to say.

"Well," Johanna said, "it's what I'm doing. There's nothing my dad can do about it."

Keti knew that was true. Although Paul Collins would certainly wish there was something he could do to stop it.

Martin awoke when Keti came to bed. He stirred and reached for her. "Are the girls in bed now?" he asked. No doubt he meant Charlotte and Johanna.

"Yes. Charlotte turned in quite some time ago."

He said, "Did they find out the sex of the baby?"

"They asked the doctor not to tell them."

"Jonah thinks he saw a penis," Martin said, with some amusement.

Keti laughed. "Well, maybe he did. There's no telling."

In the moonlight, she pulled on a white flannel nightgown and climbed into bed.

"What do you think of Grant?" she asked.

Grant had favored them with his company for about four hours the previous day, before jetting back to Manhattan. He'd discouraged Johanna from accompanying him.

"Not impressed," Martin said. Then, "Why?"

So she told him. She told him what Johanna had told her and felt sick uttering the words. "Martin, how did she become like that? She intimated... She thought I would approve of her decision. Because I'm wealthy."

"What did you say?"

"I told her I thought she'd regret it. But mostly I was dumbfounded. Still, it's her choice, and she's an adult."

"I can't believe we're going through this again," Martin said.

Again?

Keti couldn't believe it, either, if he meant what

she thought he did. "Martin, I'm not *contributing* to her doing this. I tried to discourage her. And I don't judge her. I just feel awful. Terribly sad."

"I judge her," Martin said flatly. "Keti, don't you see how your lifestyle… There are people who would do anything for it. There have been times when I thought you would."

"I think you should stop right now," she advised, "before you say something you regret."

But Martin couldn't stop. "What if it was Charlotte making that kind of choice?"

The thought of it being Charlotte was ridiculous. Charlotte was not the type and Charlotte valued people more than just about anything, except God. "I've just told you that I'm sorry it's Johanna. I think it's dreadful, and I don't want her to do it."

Martin said after a moment, "You're right. I'm so sorry—I apologize. Maybe I can just sympathize rather too well with how Paul is going to react."

"You're going to tell him." The question was stated as fact.

"I have to. What if he finds out and learns that I knew but didn't tell him?"

"Of course, it's her business. A private thing."

"But, Keti, I must give him the chance to try and stop her. Maybe *he'll* know the right thing to say. Yes, I'm going to tell him." Something seemed to occur to him. "You knew I would," he mused.

"Yes," she said. "I'd worked all that out. And I told her I would have to tell you—for much the same reason but also because you and I have no secrets from each other."

"I think, though," Martin said, "we can wait until after Christmas Day."

Chapter 15

The following year

A smaller group met at Keti's and Martin's that Christmas. Johanna's determination to marry Grant—in a wedding the following month—had caused a rift between Paul and Martin. Now it was Paul who felt that Keti's example had given his daughter skewed values.

Keti had been surprised and pleased to hear Martin tell Paul, "Keti earned her money *herself*. She never tried to marry it. She's loved me practically her whole life, just as I've loved her. Don't look to Keti for a bad example of what marriage is."

"The fact is, Johanna would never have thought that it was okay to do something like this for any amount of money, without exposure to Keti Whitechapel."

And Martin had said, coolly, "You mean Mrs. Martin Collins?"

So now they were celebrating Christmas with Charlotte, Jonah and baby Nolan, Bridget, her husband and children and *their* children, as well as Tiffany's family, but without Paul or George. George had become ardently religious and had sided with Paul in the feud. Paul's wife wanted to be part of Johanna's wedding preparations—her daughter was getting married, after all—but Paul wanted nothing to do with it and had said he wouldn't attend the service, which was to be held at St. Patrick's Cathedral in New York.

More than one person involved in the dispute had said this sort of union hardly belonged in a cathedral. Keti couldn't help feeling that she'd somehow started the feud by telling Martin what Johanna had said.

Martin said little about his brother's point of view. But he told Keti, "It's easier for Paul to think you're to blame than to wonder if he might be."

"But he's not," Keti exclaimed. "The girl likes money and power. It's that simple."

Martin, with whom her relationship had never been better, said, "Paul's her father. He's going to blame himself no matter what. But this way at least he gets to blame you out loud."

Keti knew that Martin was right.

They spent Christmas Eve holding and playing with the grandchildren—theirs and Bridget's. Keti remembered other Christmases, Christmases long gone, when she'd focused on gifts. Of course, there were gifts this year. But what Keti wanted now was to cherish those people in her life whom she loved.

She and Martin quietly went out at midnight to leave gifts of clothing, toys and money for some of the poorer families of Bounty. Keti found this to be the best part of the holiday. She and Martin had done so for the past two years, and she loved the traditions.

In previous years, Marley had accompanied them, but the old dog had finally passed away. Keti and Martin visited the pound occasionally, considering other animals, but so far Keti hadn't been able to stand the thought of a dog other than Marley in the house.

As they were walking up the path to the house quite late, Keti felt a strange tingling in her left arm. This wasn't the first time she'd noticed the sensation, and as a nurse she had a good idea about what it meant. She didn't understand where her skyrocketing blood pressure of the past few years had come from. She'd always been so healthy. Of course, since she'd gotten married she'd probably eaten richer foods than she had before. But maybe the blood pressure problem was simply genetic.

"Are you all right?" Martin asked, with uncanny awareness, as if he *knew*.

She decided to tell him about the pains. "But we don't need to rush off to the emergency room tonight."

"Actually," he said, "I disagree."

It was to be emergency surgery on Christmas Day, a quadruple bypass. As Keti lay in bed, not in the Bounty hospital but in the bigger facility in the next town, she felt gratitude that she'd suffered no heart attack before the surgery that would restore her to full health.

She would simply have to live differently now, and she was ready to do that. Things should never have come to this pass. Since Nolan's birth she'd been so happy caring for her grandson that she hadn't looked after herself as she'd previously done. Now, she would have to eat right again and insist that Martin do so, as well.

She saw none of the family but Martin before she was wheeled into surgery. The anesthesiologist smiled at her as he asked her to count backward from one hundred.

She awoke uncomfortably, aware of the tube that had assisted her breathing through the operation.

Martin was beside her, gazing down, his brown eyes dear and familiar. How strange that she, Keti

Whitechapel, had ended up married to this man, having such a *normal* life.

"Paul's been here," he said. "He says he was wrong to blame you for Johanna's choices. We've made up."

"And George?" she managed to say.

"Not yet." He smiled, and she felt his hand on hers, and she closed her eyes again.

The next Christmas

The following Christmas the whole family was together again, even Johanna and Grant, reconciled with her parents, mainly because Paul and his wife had finally agreed to take part in the wedding, which had been a huge social event.

Grant, Paul discovered on getting to know the son-in-law he hadn't wanted, enjoyed chess. Their games at this family gathering had become something of a spectator event.

"I rather like him," Keti admitted to Paul on Christmas Eve as they stood together in the kitchen washing supper dishes. Grant and Johanna had walked into Bounty to hear some madrigal singers in the park.

Paul said, "He's growing on me. But I swear I'll want to kill him if he hurts Johanna."

"Me, too," Keti said, and they smiled ruefully at each other.

Grant and Johanna returned at around ten, and the

family gathered in the living room for Christmas carols before mass.

Keti sat beside Martin and sang beside him, too, as they always had done, and she was grateful for every moment of good health they had together. She watched her grandson play under the tree with a cousin, and she closed her eyes, thinking about her blessings.

She was sixty-three. She'd survived open-heart surgery. The irony of it all, she thought, when she'd sometimes believed she had no heart. But now she and her husband still had years to enjoy together, and distant Christmases of the past, lonely Christmases, were only a memory.

She remembered the strange year of the dreams and how she had changed then, and had continued to change ever since. Martin had never been like her. His views were more rigid, more set, and he seemed to have known how he felt about most things from a young age, and not to have changed too much since then.

But together...

Together they had become as good friends, as good employers and employees, as good citizens of the world, as they knew how to be. Some people had once laughed to see the alteration in Keti and they still laughed to remember the old Keti Whitechapel. But she let them laugh and didn't give them much attention, for she was wise enough to know that nothing ever happened in life, even if it was for good, without some people somewhere finding reason to laugh, at least. Her own heart laughed with them, and she gently fingered the crystal snowflake that rested on its silver chain.

She had no further encounters with spirits, and it was said of Mr. and Mrs. Martin Collins that they knew how to keep Christmas well, if any couple alive possessed the knowledge.

* * * * *

Turn the page for a sneak preview
of the first book in the new miniseries
DIAMONDS DOWN UNDER
from Silhouette Desire®
VOWS & A VENGEFUL GROOM
by Bronwyn Jameson

Available January 2008

Silhouette Desire®
Always Powerful, Passionate and Provocative

Kimberley Blackstone didn't notice the waiting horde of media until it was too late. Flashbulbs exploded around her like a New Year's light show. She skidded to a halt, so abruptly her trailing suitcase all but overtook her.

This had to be a case of mistaken identity. Surely. Kimberley hadn't been on the paparazzi hit list for close to a decade, not since she'd estranged herself from her billionaire father and his headline-hungry diamond business.

But no, it was *her* name they called. *Her* face was the focus of a swarm of lenses that circled her like avid hornets. Her heart started to pound with fear-fueled adrenaline.

What did they want?

What was going on?

With a rising sense of bewilderment she scanned the crowd for a clue, and her gaze fastened on a tall, leonine figure forcing his way to the front. A tall, familiar figure. Her head came up in stunned recognition, and their gazes collided across the sea of heads before the cameras erupted with another barrage of flashes, this time right in her exposed face.

Blinded by the flashbulbs—and by the shock of that momentary eye-meet—Kimberley didn't realize his intent until he'd forged his way to her side, possibly by the sheer strength of his personality. She felt his arm wrap around her shoulder, pulling her into the protective shelter of his body, allowing her no time to object. No chance to lift her hands to ward him off.

In the space of a hastily drawn breath, she found herself plastered knee-to-nose against six feet two inches of hard-bodied male.

Ric Perrini.

Her lover for ten torrid weeks, her husband for ten tumultuous days.

Her ex for ten tranquil years.

After all this time, he should not have felt so familiar but, oh dear, he did. She knew the scent of that body and its lean, muscular strength. She knew its heat and its slick power and every response it could draw from hers.

She also recognized the ease with which he'd taken control of the moment and the decisiveness of his deep voice when it rumbled close to her ear. "I have a car waiting outside. Is this your only luggage?"

Kimberley nodded. "I assume you will tell me," she said tightly, "what this welcome party is all about."

"Not while the welcome party is within earshot. No."

Barking a request for the cameramen to stand aside, Perrini took her hand and pulled her into step with his ground-eating stride. Kimberley let him, because he was right, damn his arrogant, Italian-suited hide. Despite the speed with which he whisked her across the airport terminal, she could almost feel the hot breath of the pursuing media on her back.

This was neither the time nor the place for explanations. Inside his car, however, she would get answers.

Now that the initial shock had been blown away—by the haste of their retreat, by the heat of her gathering indignation, by the rush of adrenaline fired by Perrini's presence and the looming verbal battle—her brain was starting to tick over. This had to be her father's doing. And if it was a Howard Blackstone publicity ploy, then it had to be about Blackstone Diamonds, the company that ruled his life.

The knowledge made her chest tighten with a familiar ache of disillusionment.

She'd known her father would be flying in from Sydney for today's opening of the newest in his chain of exclusive, high-end jewelry boutiques. The opulent shopfront sat adjacent to the rival business where Kimberley worked. No coincidence, she thought bitterly, just as it was no coincidence that Ric Perrini was here in Auckland ushering her to his car.

Perrini was Howard Blackstone's right-hand man, second in command at Blackstone Diamonds, a legacy of his short-lived marriage to the boss's daughter. No doubt her father had sent him to fetch her; the question was *why?*

* * * * *

Get swept away down under with the glitz and glamour of the Blackstone empire as Kimberley tries to determine the real reason behind her "reunion" with Ric….

Look for
VOWS & A VENGEFUL GROOM
By Bronwyn Jameson
In stores January 2008

When Kimberley Blackstone's father is
presumed dead, Kimberley is required to take
over the helm of Blackstone Diamonds. She
has to work closely with her ex, Ric Perrini, to
battle not only the press, but also the fierce
attraction still sizzling between them. Does Ric
feel the same...or is it the power her share of
Blackstone Diamonds will provide him as he
battles for boardroom supremacy.

Look for

VOWS &
A VENGEFUL GROOM

by

BRONWYN
JAMESON

Available January wherever you buy books

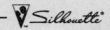

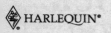

EVERLASTING LOVE™

Every great love has a story to tell™

The Valentine Gift

featuring
three deeply emotional
stories of love that stands
the test of time, just in time
for Valentine's Day!

USA TODAY bestselling author
Tara Taylor Quinn

Linda Cardillo
and
Jean Brashear

Available just in time for Valentine's Day
February wherever you buy books.

www.eHarlequin.com

HEL65427

REQUEST YOUR FREE BOOKS!

2 FREE NOVELS PLUS 2 FREE GIFTS!

EVERLASTING LOVE™

Every great love has a story to tell™

YES! Please send me 2 FREE Harlequin® Everlasting Love™ novels and my 2 FREE gifts. After receiving them, if I don't wish to receive any more books, I can return the shipping statement marked "cancel." If I don't cancel, I will receive 4 brand-new novels every other month and be billed just $4.47 per book in the U.S. or $4.99 per book in Canada, plus 25¢ shipping and handling per book and applicable taxes, if any*. That's a savings of about 15% off the cover price! I understand that accepting the 2 free books and gifts places me under no obligation to buy anything. I can always return a shipment and cancel at any time. Even if I never buy another book from Harlequin, the two free books and gifts are mine to keep forever.

153 HDN ELX4   353 HDN ELYG

Name	(PLEASE PRINT)	
Address		Apt.
City	State/Prov.	Zip/Postal Code

Signature (if under 18, a parent or guardian must sign)

Mail to the **Harlequin Reader Service®**:
IN U.S.A.: P.O. Box 1867, Buffalo, NY 14240-1867
IN CANADA: P.O. Box 609, Fort Erie, Ontario L2A 5X3

Not valid to current Harlequin Everlasting Love subscribers.

Want to try two free books from another line?
Call 1-800-873-8635 or visit www.morefreebooks.com.

* Terms and prices subject to change without notice. NY residents add applicable sales tax. Canadian residents will be charged applicable provincial taxes and GST. This offer is limited to one order per household. All orders subject to approval. Credit or debit balances in a customer's account(s) may be offset by any other outstanding balance owed by or to the customer. Please allow 4 to 6 weeks for delivery.

Your Privacy: Harlequin is committed to protecting your privacy. Our Privacy Policy is available online at www.eHarlequin.com or upon request from the Reader Service. From time to time we make our lists of customers available to reputable firms who may have a product or service of interest to you. If you would prefer we not share your name and address, please check here. ☐

HEL07

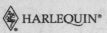

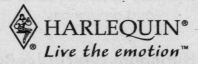